WHO, ME?

The First Book of Tanith

Jenny Sullivan

PONT

First Impression—2001

ISBN 1 85902 942 6

Printed in Wales at
Gomer Press, Llandysul, Ceredigion

Dedicated, with love,
to my brothers and sisters:
Val, Jo, David, Ruth and Nick
and also to
the latest generation:
Sophie, Ellen, Paul, Emma,
Jed, Anna Siân and Adam

Who, me? continues the story that began with the Books of Gwydion: *The Magic Apostrophe, The Island of Summer* and *Dragonson*. *The Magic Apostrophe* told how Tanith became a witch on her thirteenth birthday with the aid of a Magic Apostrophe fitted into her name – like this – 'Tan'ith'.

She was accepted into the Circle of the Daughters of the Moon, an ancient group of witches consisting of Tanith's mother and five of her six aunts. She was given a magic pendant, an emerald set in a silver five-pointed star, and the Arianrhod ring which, when touched to the green stone in the middle of the pendant, increases her magical powers.

She was also given the Emerald Spellorium, the family's Good Spell Book, and a crystal scrying ball which helps her to see what is happening elsewhere in the world. Last but not least, she was given Gwydion, a cat which can shape-shift into any creature he wishes. Gwydion's real shape, however, is human.

Tanith's Aunt Antonia keeps, locked away in a dungeon in the surprising house in which the Circle meets, the Grimoire, a Bad Spell Book, belonging to Astarte who is a member of the Perkins family of bad witches.

Astarte badly wants to get the Grimoire back so that she can have power over the earth and control and encourage wickedness and ill luck. She has a familiar, a pet magpie, and where the magpie is, Astarte is never far behind.

The Island of Summer told how Astarte and the

Great Druid managed to steal the Grimoire and take it through time to Ynys Haf, the Island of Summer, a place where magic is in every bush, tree, rock and stream, and which bears an uncanny resemblance to Wales. Tanith, Gwydion and T.A, Tanith's best friend, had to travel through the Door of Time to recover the Grimoire and bring it back.

Dragonson is the last of the *Books of Gwydion*. In it, Tanith learns why Gwydion has been called 'Dragonson' throughout the first two books. Heledd, Tanith's dingbat of a sister, has had a baby, and the dreadful Astarte Perkins, aided by Rhiryd Goch, kidnap baby Cariad and hold her to ransom. And the ransom they want, of course, is the Grimoire ... *Dragonson* also introduces Astarte's Great, Great, ever-so-many-Greats Granny. And she isn't a nice little old lady who sits in a rocking chair and knits. No. She's otherwise known as *Merch Corryn Du* – Spiderwitch.

MAIN CHARACTERS

Tanith Williams	Now sixteen and enjoying the year after GCSEs at Glanllyn comprehensive
Gwydion	Formerly a white cat – but also a Shapeshifter. Now Dragonking of Ynys Haf
Teleri Angharad Probert	Tanith's best friend – known as T.A.
Mam	Tanith's mother
The Ant	Chief Daughter of the Moon – Tanith's Aunt Antonia (and five other Aunts, who, together with Tanith, form the Circle of Seven)
Mr Howard	Tanith's School Music Teacher, who is also Taliesin, Bard and Friend to Great Merlin – but only in Ynys Haf
Heledd	Tanith's older sister
Aunty Fliss	Tanith's Aunt Felicity, now living in Ynys Haf to escape the effects of Alzheimers's Disease, a terrible disease which only affects her in the Real Time world
Nest	Gwydion's Half-Tylwyth Teg Aunt who lives in Ynys Haf
Fflur	A wolfhound who accompanied Tanith back from the Island of Summer

– AND NOT FORGETTING THE BADDIES –

Astarte Perkins	The Bad Witch
Rhiryd Goch	Evil Lord of Castell Du, who would like to be High King of Ynys Haf
The Great Druid	A Very Evil Druid, whom Tanith and Gwydion left sleeping an enchanted sleep in a cave in Ynys Haf
Merch Corryn Du	Spiderwitch – Astarte's Great-Great-Ever-so-many-Greats-Grandmother, the Wickedest Witch of All . . .

THE NEW CHARACTERS? YOU'LL MEET THEM ALL IN

Who, me?

1

All right, you try it. You wake up in the middle of the night, when it's as black as a spider's knickers in your room, something heavy is on your feet – and you can hear SOMEONE ELSE BREATHING! You'd scream too, wouldn't you? Well, I did. I started to panic even before my eyes were open (nothing wrong with a REALLY GOOD panic, that's what I think, especially when you know you are almost alone in the house!) but I calmed down when I opened them. Sitting on the end of my bed was a half-fairy. No, not half-a-fairy. That would be sick, but a half-fairy. Gwydion's Aunt Nest. Mine, too, I suppose, since we are all sort of linked by magic.

'Nest?' I said, stupidly, rubbing my eyes to get the sleep out of them. She didn't look happy. 'What's the matter? What are you doing here?'

She twisted her hair round her fingers. 'It's Gwydion. He's disappeared.'

That woke me up. 'What do you mean, he's disappeared? He's Dragonking! He isn't allowed to disappear. He's supposed to be ruling Ynys Haf, isn't he?' I sat up and stared at her.

She gazed at me. I think the expression meant, 'Pay attention, stupid.'

'Dragonking he may be, Tan'ith, but despite that and all the rest of it, he's gone.'

'But where?' I know, I know, I really was being stupid, but I still wasn't properly awake.

'If we knew where he was, he wouldn't be missing,

would he?' Nest was beginning to get exasperated, I could tell that by the way she was tearing her hair out.

'Sorry. Look, I'm awake now, honest. Nest, please. Start at the beginning, all right? What's happening in Ynys Haf? Other than Gwydion going missing, I mean.'

Nest shrugged. 'Well, no battles or anything like that. But all the same, strange stuff's been going on. I'll tell you about it . . .' she scowled '. . . when you're properly awake.'

'What about Merlin?' I asked. 'What does he think?'

Nest laughed, but it wasn't a 'funny, ha-ha' sort of laugh. 'Merlin! Fat lot of good he is in a crisis. He's gone off on one of his between-world jaunts. What a time to pick, I ask you. *And* he's taken Taliesin with him. I tried to warn Gwydion that something was up, but – well, you know Gwydion. He doesn't always pay attention.'

'You're telling me,' I said, getting out of bed and rummaging in my wardrobe for a clean pair of jeans.

'We need to get the Circle of Seven together, Tansy, and quickly,' Nest said.

That stopped me in my tracks. Well, on one foot, with the other in my jeans. 'Um,' I said, not quite knowing how to break it to her. 'That could be a bit of a problem, Nest.'

'Why? We need your mother and your aunts. Now!'

'Aunt Ant is in America, Mam is on holiday in Majorca with Dad – it's their wedding anniversary, which is why I'm here on my own except for T.A. who's sleeping in Hel's old room because she says I snore. Flissy is – well, you know where Fliss is; Aunt

12

Beulah's on safari in Africa before she gets too old, she says, Cerys is in London and Aunt Del has taken the twins to Disneyland to torture Mickey Mouse in the school holidays. So there's only me and Aunty 'Dwina out of the seven of us.'

The bedroom door slowly opened and T.A.'s tousled head peered round, her eyes bleary with sleep. 'What's going on?' she mumbled, then, 'Nest!' she shrieked, and swooped on her for a hug. 'Oh, wow!' Then she glared at me. 'You never told me Nest was coming, Tanz,' she complained. 'Meanie, keeping it to yourself.'

'I didn't keep it to myself,' I protested. 'I didn't know.'

'You must have had some idea,' T.A. grumbled, 'you always do.'

'Well, I had this weird sort of feeling something might happen, but I didn't know what.'

'You should have told me, anyway.'

'Excuse me?' Nest stood up on my bed. She was still small, as half-fairies are. Even standing on my bed she only came up to just above our head level. 'Excuse me, you two? We have a serious problem here, and you two are bickering.'

'Sorry,' I mumbled.

'Problem?' T.A. pricked up her ears. 'What problem? What's wrong?'

'Apparently Gwydion has disappeared,' I said, beginning to take in the seriousness of it for the first time. I remembered something Nest had said earlier. 'What did you mean, Nest, "strange stuff"? And what was it you warned Gwydion about?'

13

Nest sat down again, her legs crossed beneath her, like a pixie on a toadstool. 'Well, for one thing, he insisted on moving into Castell Du, even after Merlin warned him not to. Said he preferred a sea view to the mountain view he got at Castell y Ddraig, but I think it was really because Castell y Ddraig is too full of memories for him. Of his father and his Mam.'

'Why didn't Merlin want him to move into Castell Du? What's wrong with it? Now Rhiryd Goch and the Spiderwitch have been cleared out, it should be OK, shouldn't it?' I tried to remember what sort of state Castell Du had been in last time I'd seen it. Once it had been spring-cleaned, it should have been quite nice. For an old, draughty castle, that is.

'Didn't Gwydion say he was going to fill in the dungeons, get rid of the arrowslits and put nice big windows in or something?' T.A. put in.

'Mm. But do you remember what Merlin said when he suggested it? It was a long time ago, and I know your memory isn't all it used to be. Now you're old, I mean.' T.A.'s birthday is before mine, and so for two whole months she's a year older, and I like to wind her up, OK?

She scowled, and thought. Then she admitted, 'No, I don't remember. Not his exact words, anyway.'

'Well, what Merlin actually said was something like "Don't forget Castell Du is a fortress, and fortresses are built for a purpose." Oh, and something about "Just because Ynys Haf is peaceful now, don't imagine it always will be." Mmm.' I stared at Nest. 'Did Gwydion get rid of the arrowslits and put in picture windows? Do you think someone got in and captured him?'

14

Nest shook her head. 'No. He insisted on moving into Castell Du, yes, but he hadn't started remodelling the arrowslits yet. He'd filled in most of the dungeons, and he was looking at some old manuscripts to see if he could use the old Roman way of heating the place. Hippo-somethings, he called them. I thought hippos were great big river animals, but what do I know? I'm only a half fairy. I don't travel much.'

'Hypocausts,' I said absent-mindedly. 'Roman under-floor heating. So tell me, Nest, what was so strange?'

She put her small, pointed chin into her hand and considered. 'It's hard to say, exactly, Tan. He got a bit absent-minded, kept forgetting he had to be at meetings and stuff like that, and with Merlin and Taliesin off on their travels there was no one there to make him buck up his ideas. And then the girl from across the Middling Water came, and –'

'Girl? Middling Water?' I said sharply. 'What girl? What Middling Water?' Here was me hardly going out with any blokes *at all* because of Gwydion (well, one or two, maybe) and he was – well, what was he doing?

Nest flapped her hands distractedly. 'Oh, the place across the sea. Oh what is the name of it? The Land of the Giant Finn MacCuill!'

'Ireland?' T.A. and I said together.

'An Irish girl pitched up in Ynys Haf? How?' I finished.

'The way people usually get across seas,' Nest said patiently. 'By boat, of course.'

Strange, that. It had never occurred to me that people might visit Ynys Haf from other lands – except by magic, like Merlin, or through Time Doors, like us.

'So who is she?' I demanded. 'What does she want?'

'Her name is Maebh,' Nest said. 'Spelled em-ay-ee-bee-aitch but pronounced "mave". She *says* she is an Irish princess,' she frowned, 'but anyone can say she is a princess, can't she? Personally, I couldn't take to her, but Gwydion – well, you know what men are like. Believe anything if it comes from a pretty face.'

'Hmph,' I said, not liking the sound of this at all. 'And now Gwydion has disappeared, right? And where's this Maebh person? Has she disappeared, too?'

Nest nodded. 'Oh, no, she's still there. In fact, she says that as she's the only person of royal blood left in Ynys Haf, then she must automatically be Queen in Gwydion's absence!'

'She what?' I could hardly believe my ears. 'Cheeky little cow – er-slip!' I said. 'Who does she think she is?'

'Queen Maebh!' Nest and T.A. said together.

'That,' I said firmly, 'is what she thinks!'

'So what are we going to do about it?' asked T.A.

Trouble was, I didn't have a clue. And apart from me and Aunt Edwina, who had retired from being a witch when I had reached thirteen, there was no one around who could help me, except T.A. and Nest.

'I'm coming back to Ynys Haf with you, Nest.' I said firmly. 'Someone's got to sort this Maebh person out.' Then I had a thought. 'Can't we ask the Lady – ?'

Nest shook her head, firmly. 'You know as well as I do, Tan'ith, you are the Lady now. Why else do you think I'm here, for goodness sake? Who else is there?'

Put like that, there wasn't a lot I could do but get on with it. You know what they say: "when the going gets tough" – yes, I know, I usually run for cover, it's the way I'm made. But if there's no one else, well . . .

So I wrote a note to Mam and Dad, who would be back from Majorca on Sunday, posted a note through next door's letter-box asking the boy who lived there to feed and walk Fflur, my wolfhound, and got ready for a trip to Ynys Haf. Well, at least I didn't have exams to worry about – ages to go before my mock A-levels, and besides, Time is different once you get to Ynys Haf. I had to hope Heledd wouldn't try and contact me and panic when she couldn't find me, but if I let her know she would panic anyway, so I had to leave it.

'What about me?' T.A. said, hopefully.

I looked at Nest. 'Well?' I asked.

'Your decision, Tan'ith.'

'Thanks a bunch,' I muttered. 'D'you want to come, T.A.?'

'OF COURSE I DO, YOU RATBAG!' she bellowed.

Honestly, no respect! 'All right. You can come.' Actually I was going to let her come all along, but it was cool to make her suffer a bit every now and then. 'Better phone home, then, E.T.' I joked.

'Phone home? And say what? Don't worry, Ma, just popping off to a parallel universe for a bit?'

I sighed. 'Oh, come on, T.A. You're staying with me, right? Your Mam knows you're up here, so she isn't going to miss you, is she? So come on!'

We collected up everything we thought we could

17

possibly need and locked up. Mam and Dad had left the car for us, and fortunately T.A. has passed her driving test, so we weren't reduced to getting a taxi to the nearest Time Door. Come to think of it, that would have been a bit hairy, right? Please, Mr Taxi-driver, take us to the top of this bare hill right in the middle of Brechfa Forest in the middle of the night, and leave us there, OK? I don't think so.

We were half way to Brechfa when I realised I had forgotten to cancel the milk. Oh, well. Maybe the kid next door would use his brain and cancel it for us. Or at least take it off the doorstep and feed it to Fflur so it wouldn't say 'empty house, why not burgle me?' to every passing crook.

I have to say it, T.A. is a good driver. She passed her test first time, whereas I got stuck on the theory part for three goes. It wasn't that I didn't know the answers to the questions, it's just that I don't like sitting tests, right? I panic.

We took the Forestry Commission road towards the bare mountain top where the nearest Time Door stands, tucked the car away in the trees where it wouldn't be found, and began the climb. Luckily I had thought to bring torches, but even so it was hard going, because I kept tripping over bits of bramble and twig that I thought were in one place but were actually in another. At last, only a bit scratched up, we reached the summit.

I stood in the middle, Nest on my left, T.A. on my right. She was shivering with excitement.

'When we go through the Time Door,' I reminded her, 'don't let go of my hand, OK? Whatever happens, *don't let go of my hand*. And be ready for anything on the other side.'

'I r-r-remember,' she muttered, squeezing my hand painfully.

'Ow, careful!' I loosened her fingers a bit before they cut off the blood supply and my hand dropped off. 'Ready?'

We stepped forward.

2

We'd stepped forward, but just as we were about to enter the patch of shimmering air between the upright stones, I stopped, jerking my companions to a halt.

'What?' they said together.

'There's something wrong, can't you tell? I don't know what it is, but –'

T.A. shook her head, but Nest nodded, slowly.

'The stones feel wrong,' she said.

'That's it!' I knew there was something that was all wrong. 'They're facing in the other direction! We should be looking away from Carmarthen, but we aren't. We can still see the orangey glow in the sky from the street lights, right? What do you think that means, Nest?'

The half-fairy looked worried. 'I don't know. It's never happened before. It may be nothing but then . . . I think there's something dreadfully wrong.'

'So what do we do now?' T.A. asked. 'Can we try another Door?'

I thought about it, then decided it was too dangerous. 'The Doors in Time are altogether too scary to risk anything at all being wrong, no matter how small. And if one's been got at, chances are the others have, too. So what do we do now? Last time the Doors were nobbled, Gwydion and I got into Ynys Haf by the Deep Way. It was down a hole in a mountain and under the sea, I remember that much. But I haven't got a clue where it is. Oh, dammit, Nest, what can we do?'

'Let me think. There must be something.' She grabbed a lock of dark hair and munched it. 'There is another way, I know there is. I've got this vague memory of my mother's mother's mother telling me years and years ago about a fairy way into Ynys Haf. Oh, *widdershins,* what was it she said?' She sat down on the bare mountain-top, her knees tucked up under her chin, her head resting on her knees, her face hidden by her tumbling hair. T.A. and I sat beside her, quietly, letting her think. After a while, she suddenly raised her head.

'I think I remember,' she said slowly. 'It has to do with a rhyme, and I have the beginnings of it in my head already. By the time we get there, the time will be right and I shall have the rest of it. I hope,' she added.

'It's the only chance we've got. But where do we have to go?'

'To the sea,' Nest said, standing up.

'That's easy!' T.A. chortled. 'Loads of sea round here, right, Tanz?'

But Nest was shaking her head. 'Not quite as easy as that. It's a special place. And we have to get there before dawn. We can only get through at dawn. When the tide is right.'

'And there's an "R" in the month and it isn't raining, is that it?' I muttered.

'Almost. But the tides *are* right, Tan'ith, I can feel them in my blood, and if you will trust me and you will drive, T.A., we'll get there.'

I was beginning to feel a bit worried about Nest. She had risked an awful lot to cross over to this Time to tell me what was happening. Fairies – even half-

21

fairies – don't do well in human Time. They pine, and fade, and lose their powers. So apart from the other problems in Ynys Haf, I knew we had to get Nest back quickly. She was already beginning to have a sort of, I don't know, *transparent* look about her.

We walked back down the hill, backpacks seeming twice as heavy as they had when we started out, and got back into the car. T.A. put the inside light on and got out an ordnance survey map. 'Pick your beach, Nest, and I'll get us there.'

'Couldn't we shape-shift and fly wherever it is?' I suggested.

Nest shook her head. 'You could, perhaps. But I don't have the strength. My powers are almost gone. What I have I need to save, to remember the poem and get us across safely to Ynys Haf.'

She bent over the map, tucking her hair behind her ears, her small finger tracing the coastline. 'There!' she said. 'That's exactly right.'

I looked at the spot on the map where her pointing finger rested.

'Oh,' I said. 'Ah. Could be a tiny problem there, Nest.'

'What?' Nest and T.A. said together.

'Well, last time I was *there,*' I said, 'Dad had to pay for us to get in. It's Portmeirion, T.A. You know, that Italian sort of village place. I think it's all walled off and it will be locked up at night. There are bound to be security guards. How are we going to get in?'

Nest smiled. 'Don't worry,' she said. 'I can manage a little old wall and a couple of security guards. The most important part is remembering the rhyme.'

22

We drove in silence through the darkness, because Portmeirion was a fair way away, and dawn wasn't far off. But the roads were deserted, and even though I was map-reading, which I admit I am not very good at, we only got lost twice, and so we got there quite quickly. We took the turning that led down to the Portmeirion estate, tucked the car away in the car park (we'd worry about paying the parking fee later) and sneaked up to the main gate. It was closed, but there was a side road leading towards a big hotel – which I had completely forgotten was there. Obviously, there had to be access even at night for people to get in and out.

There was a security guard sitting in a dimly-lit glass booth, which gave me an anxious moment, but Nest reached into her pocket and brought out a small leather bag, which she opened. 'I'm going to sprinkle some of this on you,' she whispered. 'Don't breathe it in. It will make you sneeze.'

So we held our breaths while she sprinkled, and I waited. 'What's supposed to happen?' I whispered back.

'It already has,' she replied.

'What?'

'You're invisible.'

'I'm not!' T.A. and I whispered together.

'Yes, you are.'

'But I can still see her, and you,' I said.

'But no one else can.'

'Are you sure?'

'Look, Tan'ith, who's the fairy around here?'

'Sorry, Nest.'

I'm not kidding, we walked past that security guard,

down the hill, through the hotel grounds (OK, it was early morning and there wasn't anybody about except a kitchen worker having a sly cigarette outside the kitchen door) and down to where the fake ship was moored in the fake harbour without anyone seeing us. The tide was creeping up across the sand, and soon it would be high tide.

It was going to be a beautiful day. The sun was showing pink streaks in the east, and the moon was still out, full and transparently silver in a wonderful dark sapphire sky. I might once have thought the Lady was keeping an eye on us – but now I *am* the Lady. Not terribly comforting for a born-again coward, that.

'Right,' I said, concentrating on the job in hand, 'if you haven't remembered the rhyme, Nest, we might as well give up and go home.'

'I think I remember it,' she said. 'Take my hands and walk with me.'

Hand in hand we hopped down onto the firm, clean sand, deep swirls of tide-pools catching the pinkness of the sky. When we reached the edge of the incoming tide, Nest took a deep breath and stood at the edge of the sea, tiny, lace-edged waves whispering up to her feet.

She screwed up her eyes in concentration and began to recite.

> *'At the turn of the tide when sand is silk*
> *And sky and sea are clean and bare*
> *Find the place where light meets lightness,*
> *'Twixt sky and sea and dawn, and where*
> *there are mists, the mists of magic*

24

> *All colour leached by light and air*
> *Arch of rainbow, softest wind-rush*
> *The way to Ynys Haf is there . . .'*

When Nest reached the end of the rhyme she turned towards the rushing wind and slipping tide, and led us into the sea. I was tempted to stop and take off my trainers, since they were posh designer ones and had cost me most of my Christmas money, but I didn't need to. The tide ran *sideways* for us, sort of politely turning away, making a neat path through the water of clean sand, leaving one or two bewildered crabs and the odd flopping fish or two making a panicky dive for the retreating sea.

The sky was a curious white, almost misty colour, and there was no way of telling where the sea ended and the sky began. We walked, still hand in hand, for perhaps a quarter of an hour, an hour, perhaps several hours, for there was no feeling of time passing, and the sea curled back high over our heads, and not one drop of salt water fell on us. And then the sand began to shelve steeply upward, and through the mist appeared high cliffs. Ynys Haf!

When we reached the sandy beach, the waves closed silently behind us, and the pathway through the sea disappeared entirely.

We let go hands and looked about us. 'This feels like home,' I said, 'but which bit, I haven't a clue!'

Nest chuckled. She was looking better already. Human time didn't do her any good at all. 'We'll soon find out, once we're up there. Come on, Tan'ith, quick!' she said. 'Have you forgotten everything?'

'Birds, of course,' I said. 'What would you like to be, T.A.?'

My friend shivered in delight. 'Oh, I don't know. How about a – a – puffin?'

'The clown-face would suit you all right,' I said, 'but if we're going to fly inland, how about something a bit less obvious? You can be a puffin some other time, OK?'

I shape-shifted us into seagulls, handsome black-capped creatures with broad, strong wings, and after a tentative hop or two, and a stretch of our wings, one by one we took off and soared into the air, catching the up-draught of warmer air at the edge of the cliffs. It was so long since I'd shape-shifted, the glorious feeling of free flight almost took me by surprise.

Once aloft, we could tell where we were quite easily. On our left was the black bulk of Castell Du, its flight of black steps leading down to the jagged coast; inland in front of us, deep in the mountains, was Castell y Ddraig, and in between the two, on the edge of woodland, was the village with its chimneys smoking gently.

We soared over it, heading south, where Aunty Fliss and her husband Iestyn, headman of the village, had made their home. We couldn't head straight for either of the castles, because we didn't know where this Maebh was, for a start, and barging in like avenging angels – well, avenging seagulls, anyway – might not be a good idea. We didn't know how much magic she had, for a start. She might not have any, which would be good, but somehow, this being Ynys Haf, I didn't think we'd be that lucky.

We swooped down into the little yard outside the longhouse – the *tŷ hir* – and as I shifted back I caught the familiar smell of woodsmoke – and the midden out back, which wasn't quite so pleasant. There are definite drawbacks to medieval times!

I rapped at the door, and without waiting for a reply, stuck my head round, a big smile on my face, all prepared to be hugged and fussed over by Aunty Fliss.

Ha! I tell you, it's a good thing I'm fast on my feet! It meant I could dodge out again and shut the door before the pot that was flying through the air actually hit me!

After the crash of breaking pottery died away, I listened. There was silence inside the house, but then a little voice, sounding rather embarrassed (and so it should!) said, 'Tansy? Is that you?'

'It might be,' I said, cautiously. 'But if it's me you're throwing pots at, Aunty Fliss, then it probably isn't. Is there someone you don't want to murder? I could be her if you like.'

The door was flung open and Aunty Fliss, younger and prettier than ever (Ynys Haf has that effect on people) flung her arms around me.

'Oh, *cariad!*' she said. 'I'm sorry, I thought you were Iestyn.'

'Bit of a disagreement, Aunty Fliss?' I said, trying to keep my face straight. My Aunt and Iestyn loved each other to bits, but there was no doubt who was boss!

'Could say that,' she said, and sniffed. 'My Iestyn sometimes has a misguided sense of loyalty. That, that *woman* up at the castle, she wants him up there, to

27

take charge of the castle servants, *major domo* or something she calls it, but I've got another name for it. And he thinks he ought to do it! "Over my dead body, Iestyn," I said. If it was Gwydion asking, mind, no problem, but that Maebh person! I ask you.'

'I can't believe Iestyn would want to go and work for *her*,' Nest said, shocked. 'What's the matter with the man?'

'Oh, you know *men*,' Flissy said disgustedly. 'Show them a pretty face and their brains go out the arrowslit. But now Tan'ith is here,' she smiled, brushing a feather from my shoulder, 'you'll sort everything out, won't you, lovely girl?'

'Who, me?' I said.

3

'Well, of course you!' Aunty Fliss and Nest said together. 'If Gwydion isn't here, then the Lady takes over. Everyone knows that!'

'Oh,' I said, a bit uncertainly. 'Trouble is, I'm not quite sure where to start. Find this Maebh person, I suppose, and ask her what she thinks she's doing.'

'Oh, she knows perfectly well what she's doing,' Aunt Fliss said crossly. 'What she's doing is trying to take over Ynys Haf when she's no right. She just wandered in one day without so much as a by-your-leave, made eyes at that stupid boy and that was it. Honoured guest, she was. Banquets and minstrels and all sorts. Men. They're hopeless. And my Iestyn's just as bad.'

Right on cue, almost as if Aunt Fliss's words had summoned him, the door of the *tŷ hir* inched open, and Iestyn's worried face peered round it. This time, luckily, Aunty Fliss didn't have a pot handy. When he saw Nest, T.A., and me his face lit up.

'Ah. Tan'ith. Welcome home, *ferch,* Now we'll get something done, look!'

'Ha!' Fliss snorted. 'You've changed your tune.'

'Well, with Gwydion gone, I was all of a fuddle, *ben-i-lawr,* topsy-turvy. Didn't know what to do for the best, me being head of the village and all. Got to be someone in charge, stands to reason, and it couldn't be me taking over all of Ynys Haf, wouldn't be right, me not being anybody in particular.'

29

'You've got as much right as that Maebh!' Aunt Fliss said indignantly. 'All right for you to be *major domo* up at the Castle for that – that *baggage,* though, I suppose!'

Iestyn sighed. 'Now if you'd listened, my lovely, instead of flying off the handle like you did and chucking pots at my head, you would have heard me say that *if* I took the job that was offered me, *if* mark you, not *when*, I'd be right well placed to keep an eye on that young madam up the Castle.'

'Oh,' Fliss said, her voice rather small. 'Oh, I see.'

Iestyn knew when to press his advantage. 'But no,' he went on, 'you had to jump to conclusions and start chucking stuff about.' He picked up the scattered shards of the pot that had just missed me. 'And this looks like that nice handy ewer I paid a good few coppers for at the market last week.'

Aunt Fliss looked as if she wanted to say sorry, but couldn't quite manage it. 'Well, you should have said,' she said crossly instead. 'Am I supposed to be a mind-reader?'

T.A. looked at me and we grinned at each other. Just like being at home, really. Mam and Dad occasionally had 'discussions' like this, and Mam never apologised, either. Perhaps it was a family thing.

'Anyway,' Nest said briskly. 'Tan'ith is here now, so what are we going to do?'

And they all looked at me expectantly.

'Um,' I said. 'I'd love a cup of tea.'

'Have to be rose-hip or blackberry,' Fliss said, 'unless . . .?'

T.A. beamed and unslung her backpack. 'Teabags,

Aunt Fliss. I ask you, would we come to visit you without bringing prezzies?'

We unloaded tea-bags, and instant coffee, and baked beans and perfumed bath-foam, and loo-roll, and all the other stuff that Aunt Fliss missed so much, while Nest raised her eyes to heaven and sighed.

'Honestly, Fliss, I don't know why you don't magic yourself some of this stuff if you want it.'

'You know perfectly well why not,' Fliss said, going red about the ears. 'I just don't think it's right to be in a place and not live the same as everyone else.'

'But it's different when it's a present,' Iestyn said, reaching happily for the jar of sandwich spread T.A. had just produced. Iestyn had discovered sandwich spread last time T.A. had brought a goodie-bag, and had got hooked straight away. So we feasted, and I had my cup of tea, and then we sat round the table amid the empty packets and beakers (we managed to find one each that Fliss hadn't broken!) and got serious.

'So,' I said. 'This Maebh person. What's she like?'

'I've only got glimpses of her,' Fliss said, licking butter from her fingers, 'but Iestyn here was *summoned*.' She said 'summoned' the way a person might say 'smallpox', or 'headlice'.

Iestyn frowned at his wife. 'And I went, Fliss, for the good of my community. And if it helps the Lady here to get Gwydion back and get rid of the Irishwoman, then it will be worth spending a few hours a day in her company.'

It still felt weird being referred to as the 'Lady'. The Lady, to my mind, was still the mysterious, slim, beautiful, star-hung vision that I had first seen in Aunt

Ant's special room. Not me, at all. But the Lady had passed her magic to me. I had to use it, use it wisely, and use it for Ynys Haf. I straightened my back and looked earnest.

'You tell me, Iestyn, please.'

He frowned, his wind-burned face collapsing into deep grooves around his chin. 'She's comely, Lady, no doubt about that. Pretty to make birds fall out of trees and dogs forget to bark, with her lovely black hair, and her blue eyes and her skin like cream, and the height of her.'

'Hmmph!' said Aunty Fliss.

I knew what she meant. Speaking as a shortish, skinnyish, freckledy, red – no, *auburn*-haired person, I hated her already. 'Tall, is she?' I asked glumly.

'Aye, tall for a woman in these parts, I suppose. Comes up to Gwydion's shoulder. Mind, he's growed since you last saw him, Lady. Tops any man in Ynys Haf these days.'

Since Gwydion had been well over six feet tall when I last saw him, I wondered how big he was now! I felt a sudden pain of loss – oh Gwyd, where are you? I wondered – but pushed it out of my mind. First things first. Check out this Irish person, and try to find out where Gwydion had gone. I could measure him later, when I'd found him.

'I suppose you've tried scrying for him, have you?' I suggested. 'It's amazing what you can pick up from a good crystal ball.'

Nest gave me a Look. 'Of course we have. We've scryed in glass and we've scryed in water and we've scryed indoors and we've scryed outdoors and up

32

mountains and by the rivers and by the sea. We've scryed until we are purple in the face. But wherever he is, we can't see him.'

'Perhaps if the Lady has a go . . .?' Iestyn suggested quietly. 'She has the greatest powers, after all.'

I shrugged. 'It's worth a try, I suppose.'

Nest brought her scrying-bowl: dark wood, carved on the outside with strange and wonderful carvings, smooth as black glass inside, and filled it with clear water from the spring. When the water had stilled and was calm and mirror-like, I looked into it, concentrating as hard as I could, but all that I could see was blackness and my own reflection.

Then, remembering something I'd read in the Spellorium, I blew softly on the water and magically, as the surface rippled under my breath, smoke obscured the bowl. When I blew it away, it rose into the air, fragrant, spicy, clean-smelling. When it cleared, I looked again into the scrying bowl. At first I thought that my longing to see Gwydion had made me imagine it, but then the image became clearer, and I could see a tall figure lying motionless on a bed. I bent closer, trying to make out the face, and obligingly, the scrying-bowl's zoom lens seemed to go into operation, because I instantly had a close-up.

It was Gwydion, and he was fast asleep. I could see his chest rise and fall with his even, peaceful breathing.

'Well,' I said indignantly. 'He's all right then. Dead to the world. Certainly not in any hurry to get away and come home, is he?'

'But where is he, Tansy?' asked Fliss.

I bent over, and looked again, then drew my head back. Sure enough, the picture in the bowl drew back, widened out, so that I could see Gwydion's surroundings. He lay on a bed, yes, but he was in some sort of cave with rough walls of rock. The remains of a tray of food lay on the floor, a wine goblet tipped, sending a few crimson drops across the floor.

'Look at him,' Nest said. 'He's lying too still. I don't think he's asleep. He's unconscious.'

Somehow, that made me feel better and worse, both at the same time! 'Unconscious? How can you tell?'

'It's just that he's so still. You forget, Tan'ith, I have known Gwydion since he was a tiny boy, when his Mam died. Indeed, until he went to Merlin's tower when he was eight, I was his nurse. I know how he sleeps. He's always been restless, kicking off the covers, tossing, turning. But look at him now. He's completely still except for the breath in and out of his lungs. He is drugged, Tansy. Or enchanted.'

'Likely enchanted,' Iestyn said, from his place against the wall and well away from the magic business. Non-magical people in Ynys Haf had a healthy respect for the magical ones. 'Likely that woman has put a spell on him.'

'I wish we could find out where he is,' I muttered. 'Then we could go and get him. He'd know what to do. Gwyd may not always be right, but at least he always has some ideas to start work with.'

'And so will you, Tan'ith,' Aunt Fliss said gently. 'You have the power. Listen to it, child. Listen hard. Listen to the sounds of Ynys Haf. Take time, remember what it is like to be here. Get the twentieth – no, it's the twenty-first century back there, now, isn't it? – get the modern days out of your heart and soul and breathe in the air of Ynys Haf. It will give you strength.'

'Flissy is right, Tanz,' T.A. put in unexpectedly. 'This place is so different you need to get used to it again. No use blundering about in a hurry and getting it all wrong.'

I just felt miserable. 'I know. I hear what you are saying, all of you, but it's scary being responsible for all this. Being the Lady and everything, and Gwydion being in trouble, and some strange female moving in and taking over, just like that. And I've only just finished my GCSE's!' I wailed.

That did it. Aunt Flissy's face twitched, Nest hid a smile behind her hand and T.A. guffawed loudly. Even Iestyn chortled, and he didn't have a clue what a GCSE was!

'You'll be telling us next that you have your mock A's to worry about!' T.A. teased. 'Ooh, diddums den! Come on, Tanz, don't be such a wimp. You're the Lady. You can do it.'

I wasn't convinced.

4

What they said made sense. I needed to get the feel of Ynys Haf back inside me, so that I could hear what was happening around me.

'I'm going for a walk,' I said. 'Coming, T.A.?'

'You bet,' she said. 'Um – I think we ought to change our clothes, Tanz. We're going to stick out like sore thumbs in jeans and trainers, right?'

'Oh, right,' I said, and giggled. 'What do you fancy, T.A.? Velvet? Silk?'

'You'd do better in a nice bit of homespun,' Iestyn said disapprovingly. 'Shouldn't ought to go wandering around looking like you're all dressed up for a Michaelmas market.'

'He's boring, but right,' Aunt Flissy said. 'If I were you, I'd probably go for a nice pair of breeches and a warm tunic. That way you can go where you want without worrying about getting dresses caught on brambles.'

So I concentrated very hard and dressed T.A. and myself in leather breeches, homespun tunics and boots. 'What's the weather like, Iestyn?' I asked.

He glanced out of the window. 'Sunny, looks like.'

'Yes, but what time of the year is it? It's May in our time. Sometimes Ynys Haf is a bit behind or a bit ahead. The first time it was winter and we nearly died of frostbite.'

'It's May, I think,' Iestyn said uncertainly. 'I get mixed up, sometimes. I go by the season, not the month. Late spring, anyway.'

36

So I magicked us some warm woollen cloaks, just in case.

'While you are out,' Nest said, 'better go and tell the bees you're back.'

I had almost forgotten the bees. They like to know what's going on with their people.

We slipped out of the house and looked around. Nothing had changed since last time. Above the trees in the distance, thin plumes of smoke rose into a clear blue sky.

We went round to the back of the *tŷ hir* to where the bees hummed in and out of four spanking new wood-and-reed hives. Walking slowly, so as not to frighten them, I went to kneel in front of the neat row – almost like small, round detached houses. 'Excuse me, bees,' I began, one ear listening for T.A. to giggle. 'I just popped round to tell you that I'm back in Ynys Haf.' The gentle, sleepy buzzing from the hives seemed to have quietened. 'You helped me last time I was here, and I haven't forgotten. I'll tell you everything that's going on, I promise.' There, that was done.

Before I could stand up and glare at T.A. just in case she was even thinking of laughing, two handsome fat bees flew out of each hive. They flew around my head like the little planes that buzzed King Kong at the end of the film, as if they were inspecting me. I waited until they flew back into the hives and the buzz went back to its former volume, and then turned round. T.A. wasn't laughing.

'Those bees,' she said, 'whizzing round your head like that. They looked like a little flying crown!'

'They were just making sure who I was, that's all,' I

said. 'Come on, let's go. We won't go near the village; I don't want to meet anyone, not yet.'

We ambled slowly through the wood. The bluebells were out, a whispering carpet of sapphire, so it was probably closer to the end of April than the end of May.

T.A. chuckled. 'I wonder if Sion ap Sion is still around, Tanz? Remember his great big, droopy moustache?'

I lowered my voice, imitating Sion. '"Her's got shorten 'air, an' spotty dapples on 'er face"' I quoted. 'Cheeky so-and-so. Still, by the time Gwydion was crowned Dragonking, he'd sort of got to like me, hadn't he?'

'Do you mean "Got to" in the sense of couldn't help it, he had to or Gwydion would have clouted him one, or "got to" in the sense of "had become fond of you", Tanz?' T.A. asked solemnly.

I gave her a poke in the ribs. 'Stop teasing, T.A.'

She did a mock bow. 'Yes, your Ladyship.'

I wanted to prod her again, but something had caught my eye. 'Shh!' Quickly I grabbed her arm and pulled her behind a tree. 'Look!' I whispered. '*Look, T.A.!*'

She looked, and stepped further back into the tree-line, her eyes wide with disbelief, as my own probably were. It was almost like stepping back in time. Riding past us was a short, stocky, fox-haired man, a longbow and a quiver of arrows on his back, a vicious spear in his right hand.

When he had ridden past, I stared at T.A. 'Rhiryd Goch!' I whispered. 'But it can't be!'

'Not unless Spiderwitch failed when she tried to drown him,' T.A. said, but her face was pale, and I could see that she was having trouble believing her own eyes, just as I was.

'Spiderwitch let him burrow into her cavern to rescue her, right? He drowned, just as she knew he would, didn't he? There wasn't any doubt about that at all.'

T.A. said slowly, 'I didn't actually see his body, Tanz, but I think everyone sort of agreed that yes, he had actually popped his clogs.'

'Well, either we're seeing ghosts, T.A., or he didn't drown. And if Rhiryd Goch is back, then there is definitely something weird happening here.'

We sort of lost interest in going walkabout then, and headed (fairly fast) back to the *tŷ hir*, not particularly wanting to bump into any other raves from the grave, which is what Rhiryd Goch had to be. Didn't he?

By the time we got back the sun was going down, and a wonderful smell of cooking meat drifted on the wind towards us. It smells wonderful *now*, I reminded myself, but by the time I left Ynys Haf I'd probably be thoroughly fed up with rabbit, venison and wild boar stew and dying for a Big Mac and fries. We burst into the smoky, darkening room just as Nest was lighting the rushlights. Pooh. I'd forgotten what a treat they were, too! They absolutely stank. Still, I suppose if you have no choice but to use mutton fat for lighting – beeswax candles were much too expensive for every day – the pong was only to be expected.

'Nest, Fliss,' I said as we arrived, 'I'm absolutely

positive T.A. and I have just seen Rhiryd Goch! Didn't he drown, after all?'

'Oh yes, he drowned,' Nest said, blowing out the taper she had used. 'You didn't see Rhiryd Goch. You saw his son.'

'Rhiryd had a son? Oh no. Is he like his father?'

'In looks or in manners?'

'Well, we know he looks like him,' I said. 'Mam would say he is the "spit out of his mouth". But is he *like* him?'

'Oh yes,' Flissy said grimly. 'Rhiryd ap Rhiryd is the very image of his father. And so are Ardwyn ap Rhiryd and Jason ap Rhiryd, his brothers.'

'Jason?' I said, weakly.

'Jason,' Nest said, grinning. 'His Mam liked it, apparently. Heard it in a story once, some visiting bard. She said it was all about golden fleas, and she decided that golden fleas had to be better than the ordinary black sort, even if they did still bite. She was that type of woman, though. Full of flights of fancy, and pretty, as well. Goodness knows why she married him.'

'Do they all look the same? Like Rhiryd Goch, I mean.'

Nest shook her head. 'No, only Rhiryd looks like Rhiryd. Ardwyn and Jason look like twin weasels. Fair-headed, they are, like their Mam was, but their eyes are set too close together, and they are thin as sticks and like as two peas in a pod. But they all have their Dada's nature, that's for certain. You'd do well to keep away from them if possible.'

'I didn't know Rhiryd Goch had a wife, let alone a family,' I said, weakly.

40

'Oh, yes,' Iestyn was lounging beside the fire, toasting his toes. 'Nice little wife; too good for him, like Nest says. Didn't ask to be married to Rhiryd Goch, but her father insisted. And then she died. But she gave him young Rhiryd and the twins before she popped off.'

'So where have they been until now?' T.A. asked.

'Oh, round and about. Just as Gwydion was apprenticed to Merlin when he was eight, those three were sent off as well. Their grandfather has estates in the Out Isles, up beyond the Lost Lands. Anyway, the boys came back to lay claim to Castell Du, apparently, but Gwyd soon saw them off. Told them to count themselves lucky he didn't lock them up in his dungeons. Only he couldn't have done, he was only threatening, because he'd filled them in by then. The dungeons, I mean.'

'Out Isles? Beyond the Lost Lands?' T.A. asked, bemused.

'The Out Isles are the top bit of Scotland. The Orkneys, Shetland, places round there,' I said, wondering how I knew. 'And the Lost Lands is England. Tell me,' I said, 'just for the interest, but when did they come back? About the same time as Maebh arrived, or before?'

Iestyn sat up, slowly. 'Now you mention it, *ferch*, it was about the same time – or a little bit before. Wasn't it, Fliss?'

Flissy stopped stirring the pot and nodded. 'You're right. I've never put the two things together in my mind before, but – yes. A couple of weeks before Maebh swanned in, they sort of appeared. And then

41

Her Gorgeousness started throwing her charm about and everyone sort of forgot Rhiryd ap Rhiryd and his brothers.'

'Hmm.' Something was beginning to turn, although very slowly, in my mind. 'Aunt Fliss, you've been a witch longer than I have. I know Wales is magical, but what about Scotland? And Ireland? And is there anywhere else?'

Fliss laughed. 'Magic is everywhere, *cariad*, you know that. But there are places where the people believe in it more, which makes it stronger, and the gap between magic and not-magic closes until it's barely there at all. The Out Isles, yes, and Ireland, Brittany and Cornwall, and the Isle of Man – all the Celtic and Gaelic nations.'

'So,' I chewed my little fingernail, the one I keep specially for the purpose. 'So, let's get this straight. Gwydion disappears shortly after these three blokes arrive from the Out Isles, and shortly after that Madame Maebh arrives from Ireland? So now we have Rhiryd Goch's three sons plus this Maebh person, right? Bit coincidental, isn't it?'

Iestyn stared at me. 'She brought someone else with her, too. A little oily Irishman by the name of Henbane. He's sort of her – I don't know, her adviser, I suppose. He's always at her elbow, anyway.' He ran his fingers through his hair, making it stick up. 'Oh, Fliss, I know you don't want me to have anything to do with that woman, but don't you see it would be a perfect way to keep an eye on her and discover what is going on?'

Flissy sighed. 'Oh, I know, I know. You're right,

Iestyn. But I – I don't want you getting hurt. I don't want you mixed up in trouble. You got locked up in a dungeon last time, and it was Rhiryd Goch that did that. His sons are just as bad as he was.'

'But I can't just do nothing, love. I'm the –'

'I know. You're the head man around here,' Fliss said exasperatedly. 'Look, supper's ready. Come and eat and I'll think about it.'

It really would be a wonderful opportunity having someone like Iestyn up at Castell Du keeping an eye on what was going on up there. He might be able to hear something, find out where Gwydion was. I opened my mouth to urge Fliss to agree to Iestyn becoming major whatsit up there, and then T.A. dug me in the ribs, reading my mind, and I shut it again.

'Let Flissy decide, Tanz,' she whispered. 'You may be the Lady, but he's her husband.'

Of course, Fliss decided that he should go. She was one of the Seven, after all, even if the other five were currently scattered all over the place at the most inconvenient time possible.

And so, next morning, Iestyn put on his best tunic and cloak, pulled a woolly hat down over his hair, climbed on his horse and set off to Castell Du.

What he didn't know, however, and what Flissy did, when she calmly straightened his collar and kissed him goodbye, was that I was going with him, which was why Fliss was so calm and good-natured and unflappy about the whole thing!

Just before he left I wished him luck and disappeared up the ladder to the sleeping loft, and made loud bed-making noises. However, just as he

43

pulled on the woolly hat I shape-shifted, flew down, perched on top of it, and rode on it all the way to Castell Du. After all, it takes very good eyesight to spot a ladybird approaching from above, and Iestyn was a trusting soul. He was also not very good at keeping secrets, which is why Fliss, Nest and I didn't tell him he would have company on his visit to Castell Du.

Ladybugs, however, are a bit on the vulnerable side when it comes to birds, so I tucked myself away out of sight in the rolled up hat-brim, and had a bit of a snooze (well, I'd got up EARLY!) until I felt him lurch out of the saddle and down onto cobblestones. Then I crawled out, flew from his hat to his collar (I knew the hat would come off as soon as he met a lady of any description: a real gent, our Iestyn!) and sat there, out of sight, watching everything that was going on.

Iestyn handed his mount over to a stable-hand, and, ducking his head, went through the courtyard door into the Great Hall. The big, shadowy room looked just as it had in Rhiryd Goch's day: men-at-arms lounging around, or eating, or playing cards, or stringing bows or making arrows.

And then I saw a face I recognised. It was a girl, and she was carrying a tray of beakers. A man, sitting down at a table with friends, had his arm round her waist in a friendly way – too friendly, if you ask me, I'd have thumped him one – and she was flirting with him. I racked my brains trying to remember who she was. And then it came to me. It was Mali, the laundry-girl, whom I had bamboozled into believing that I had given her a love-potion, as a reward for getting us into the castle last time. So, she wasn't washing the men-at-arms' smelly socks any more. Last I'd heard, she'd been going to marry Dafydd ap Rhodri . . . I filed it away to mention to Nest and Fliss. They'd know all the gossip. If Iestyn got the job as chief steward, that was two people working for us inside Castell Du. If Mali could still be trusted.

Iestyn was greeted by a short man, with black shiny hair tied back in a bunch at the nape of his neck. He was quite handsome in a slimy sort of way.

'Ah,' he said, 'Iestyn. And have you reconsidered Queen Maebh's offer at all?' His Irish accent sounded strange in the great hall of Castell Du.

Iestyn's hat came off, as expected. He twisted it in his hands, nervously. Obviously not good at being a spy, our Iestyn. 'I have, Master Henbane. I have decided that it-will-be-an-honour-to-serve-er-um,' he said. He couldn't quite bring himself to say 'the Queen'.

Despite Master Henbane's apparently welcoming smile, his lips were thin and mean. 'Her Majesty will be pleased, and I confess I shall be relieved to have the running of this great barn taken from my shoulders. I have more – aah – *important* things to consider. Follow me.' And he strode off down a corridor, with Iestyn scurrying like White Rabbit behind. Oh, and me, of course, sitting on his collar, holding on with all six of my feet.

Master Henbane opened a door and stood back. 'Iestyn, Majesty.'

And I saw Maebh for the first time.

5

She was the sort of person who makes me want to slap them, very hard. Oh, she was pretty, I suppose I have to give her that, but it was a sort of 'oh, I'm so sweet and helpless' type of prettiness.

She wore a long gown of pink silky stuff, with so many ruffles, twiddly bits and bows that she looked like one of those naff frilly covers for spare toilet rolls you sometimes see in old ladies' bathrooms. Her hair was so dark it was almost black, and it shone with bluish highlights. She had huge blue eyes, dark lashes and skin so white that she looked almost ghostly, but not in the slightest bit spooky. She had deep dimples, which she flashed at Iestyn, who almost tied himself into knots; and fluttery little hands. See what I mean? I'm not a violent person, but she really, really made me want to smack her. And she was tall and slim, and didn't have a freckle anywhere, as far as I could see.

'Oh,' she trilled (and I mean *trilled*: her voice was like birdsong) 'oh, Master Henbane dear, has Iestyn agreed to be Our *Major Domo*?'

(Our? Who did she think she was, the Queen? Oh. Yes, she did.)

Master Henbane bowed low, pointing his toe in front of him. 'Ah, Majesty,' he purred, 'the day has turned to sunshine, to be sure. Your wish is granted. Iestyn has agreed to forsake his duties as Head Person of the Village and become *Major Domo* of Castell Du.'

During all this general smarminess Iestyn was

twisting his cap as if he were trying to wring it out. I was quite glad I'd made for the safer region of his collar.

Maebh clasped her fluttery hands in front of her chest and gazed at him. The dark lashes slithered down over the blue eyes and Iestyn went a deeper shade of pink. 'Oh thank you, thank you!' she cried. 'I shall feel so safe with you in charge, dear Iestyn!'

I ask you, what was she like? She talked like a reject from a Jane Austen novel! Only with an Irish accent, begorrah and bewhatsit!

Iestyn mumbled something and turned bright red. I began to worry about him spontaneously combusting, but once he had bowed (Iestyn, bowing!) and Maebh had allowed him to kiss her hand, Master Henbane hustled him out of the room, closing the door behind him.

Iestyn's colour was beginning to subside, thank goodness. I hoped it would be completely back to normal before he got back to the *tŷ hir,* or Aunty Fliss would have a word to say. Many words, probably.

'Iestyn,' the slimy little man began. 'You will begin your duties tomorrow. You will be here at dawn to serve Her Majesty's breakfast, which should be two soft-boiled eggs – speckledy brown ones – with fresh brown bread and butter cut in soldiers no more than one inch wide. After that you will stand behind her Majesty's chair while she holds court.' Master Henbane clicked his fingers, and a tall man appeared from the shadows. 'Seamus, will you see to it that Iestyn is fitted out with suitable clothing. Iestyn, you will always wear your uniform in Her Majesty's presence. You will be paid monthly if your work is satisfactory. You will be on call night and day from dawn tomorrow. Do you understand me now?'

'Night and day?' Iestyn gasped. 'But I –'

'Night and day,' Master Henbane repeated, his eyes glittering.

My temper started to bubble a bit. Dancing attendance on the Jane Austen reject would mean Iestyn wouldn't be able to see Aunty Fliss or sort out the villagers' problems or anything. Not only that, I think Iestyn had missed the bit about 'paid monthly *if* your work is satisfactory'! That could mean not a lot of pay coming his way, since I didn't particularly trust Henbane. Still, it was in a good cause – Iestyn would be our spy at Castell Du. I should have to shape-shift and go to him to find out anything he'd discovered, though, because it looked as if he wouldn't be able to get to us, not if he was working round the clock.

'Um?' Iestyn muttered, strangling the woolly hat again, 'beggin' your pardon, Master Henbane, but won't I be having any time off?'

'Time off?' Master Henbane smiled. It wasn't a nice smile, it just the drawing back of thin, thin lips from small, sharp teeth. 'Time *offfff?* Of course. You shall have off Midsummer Day, one of the Equinoxes, and August Bank Holiday. Unless, of course, Her Majesty needs you or the day in question falls on a Monday, Friday or Saturday. Now you may go. Don't be late tomorrow.'

Iestyn, as pale now as he had once been scarlet, followed Seamus out of the door and across the courtyard.

I was not with him. As Iestyn had turned to go, I leapt off his collar and landed on Master Henbane's. Seconds later I was face to face with Maebh again. She was sitting on her throne munching candied fruit from a large bowl on the table beside her throne. I hoped they gave her zits and tooth-rot.

'Did I do well, Master Henbane? Is the village Ours, and all the people in it?'

'It is, so, your Majesty. All that you have to do now is visit the peasants, and the entire population will worship you. It is only a matter of time before Ynys Haf is ours.'

'Mine,' Maebh trilled, her eyelashes fluttering. 'You said I could be Queen.'

'As you say, Your Gloriousness.' Henbane bowed a smarmy bow.

I suppose it would be a bit obvious for a ladybird to say I 'saw red' but I did. I wanted to turn into a wasp and sting them both. But I stayed still and tried to keep calm. I had to learn as much as I possibly could. I already knew they were up to no good. Oh, Gwydion, *where are you?* I thought.

'Henbane?'

'Yes, your Adorable Exquisiteness?'

'Can you not feel something strange?'

Henbane put his head on one side. 'Strange, O Wondrous One?

'Really strange, Henbane. If I didn't know better, I'd almost think I could feel a goodwitch somewhere close. That is impossible, isn't it, Henbane? You have taken care of the goodwitches? I don't like them. They frighten me.' She shuddered, attractively.

49

'Most certainly, your Majesty. All the Time Doors are – shall we say out of order?' He chuckled. It wasn't a happy sound. 'As soon as one of the Daughters of the Moon tries to step across from that Time to this one, phhhhhht! Instant annihilation.'

Maebh clutched herself, happily. 'Oh, I like the sound of that, Henbane, I do so. Instant anny- what you said.'

That, I thought grimly, *is what you think, your dimwittedness.* I had just decided it was time to make like yesterday and begone when Maebh spoke again.

'Keep very still, Henbane.'

Henbane froze, staring warily at her. 'Why?'

'"Why, your Majesty", Henbane. There's a wee red beetle on your collar.' And she shot out her fingers and grabbed at me. I only just made it. I hurled myself off Henbane's collar, flew frantically for the nearest arrow-slit and out into the courtyard. I thought I had made it, but I glanced over my shoulder (or whatever passes for a shoulder in a ladybird) and saw Maebh staring out of the window. Suddenly, her outline sort of shimmered . . .

And *shifted*.

Maebh was a witch!

And guess what she shifted into? A large, very familiar-looking magpie.

You know that 'oh, heck, I've been here before' sort of feeling? *Déjà vu* the French call it. But it was impossible. Up until now, through all my trials and traumas as a good witch, wherever the magpie had been, Astarte my arch-enemy, had never been far behind. But I knew that Astarte Perkins had been dealt

50

with once and for all. First I had de-magicked her, and then I had turned her into a frog. There was no way she could have got out of that spell. No way at all, trust me. And yet – here was her magpie. I was beginning to feel a bit discombobulated: first Rhiryd ap Rhiryd, now the blooming magpie! What next? Then, rapidly, there were more urgent things on my mind.

The magpie was gaining on me, its sharp beak open wide. And I didn't want to be a magpie's breakfast. I also didn't want to let on that I was me, if you see what I mean, so shape-shifting was right out of it. I had to cope with this as a ladybird. A ladybird with a brain, admittedly, but still, a very small ladybug. The magpie was getting closer, and closer, and –

And from nowhere at all a small squadron of fat honey-bees turned up and surrounded me, confusing the magpie with their sheer numbers, and guided me swiftly into a hole in a tree that I should never have spotted without them.

The magpie gave up looking for me after a while, and flew back in through the arrowslit. Before I left the hole, though, I changed into a sparrow and, accompanied by my bee escort, flew back to the *tŷ hir*.

Outside the familiar wooden door I shimmered and shifted into myself, and lifted the latch. There was a bit of an Atmosphere inside: Aunty Fliss had a face like what Mam would have called a slapped bottom, Nest was stirring the cauldron over the fire very vigorously indeed, and was in danger of turning the venison stew (again) to minced meat soup.

Iestyn, clutching a pile of expensive looking velvet,

51

stood beside the table. He didn't look exactly happy, either. From the sounds that came from the cow-byre at the other end of the long-house, T.A. was lurking there, probably rediscovering her milking skills and hiding out at the same time.

'What's going on?' I asked, and was surprised to find that my voice came out rather crossly. Aunty Fliss glared at Iestyn.

'Bad enough him dancing attendance on that woman, without her dressing him up like a fourpenny dinner.'

'It's a uniform, Flissy,' Iestyn muttered. 'You want me there, spying, I got to wear the uniform, right? Anyone would think I wanted to do it. Can't have time off, got to take her breakfast, what does the woman think I am, a chambermaid?'

'He's right, Flissy,' I said briskly. 'We need Iestyn to spy for us. Don't you realise how much he's risking for us all?'

'Oh, don't you think I haven't worried about that?' Aunty Fliss wailed, and burst into tears. 'Maybe she's just what she says she is, an Irish princess who has a right to be Queen since Gwydion's gone. Maybe we just ought to let her take over. Someone has to do it, after all.'

Nest turned from her cauldron to stare at her. 'I don't believe you said that, Flissy! She has no right. If Gwydion is not here, for whatever reason, then you know as well as I do that only Tan'ith has the right to rule.'

'Who, me?' I said, stupidly.

'Oh, for goodness sake,' Nest said, and threw the ladle at the wall. Being made of wood it clattered a bit, and a chip of wood flew out of it. 'What is the matter with you, Tan'ith? You know you are the Lady. You know you are destined to be here with Gwydion –'

'Me? With Gwydion?'

'Of course.'

'But what about my A-levels? College?' I said.

'If everything had gone as it should, then you would be still in your Time, worrying about such stupid little mortal problems. But Gwydion has disappeared, and so Ynys Haf needs you. Everything else takes second place. And if we don't find Gwydion, then you are here forever.'

Don't know why I bothered to say anything, really. I knew perfectly well what the situation was. T.A. appeared in the doorway, her face pale, and I didn't feel too rosy myself. I knew Nest was right. I knew that my place was here in Ynys Haf – but there were things I wanted to do in the twenty-first century that I couldn't do here. The great big word 'Duty' seemed to have come out of nowhere, and I didn't like it at all.

'Then we must find Gwydion,' I said, as resolutely as I could. 'But in the meantime, Flissy,' I said sternly, 'I'm afraid that you will have to bear being without Iestyn. You must stop making him feel bad about being at Castell Du. If he's worrying about you all the time, then he will be useless to us.'

Flissy opened and shut her mouth, and Nest and T.A. stared at me. I was a bit surprised myself, taking charge like that. But I had to do it: it felt right.

'Come on,' I said, 'let's have a quick snack and then we must talk. Rather a lot happened after you left, Iestyn.'

6

After a fast lunch of bread, apples and sharp, crumbly white cheese, I helped T.A. clear away and rinse the wooden dishes in the water-trough. We sent Iestyn off to the village to explain what was happening, and the rest of us sat around the table with cups of hot tea.

I fished out my soggy tea-bag, whizzed it out the window (what a fright that would give a future archaeologist!) and quickly brought them up to date with what had happened. When I got to the bit about the magpie, they all stared at me open-mouthed.

'Astarte Perkins can't be back!' Flissy said. 'It's impossible. She had no magic at all, it was all gone. She was a frog, for goodness sake! Frogs – even ex-witch type frogs – don't have enough brain to shape-shift.'

'I know that. But I've been thinking. Let me run a couple of ideas past you. Supposing – just supposing, mind – that when Astarte's magic left her, it went into her magpie?'

Nest shook her head. 'Couldn't happen. When magic is taken out of someone it disperses – a bit like smoke – or toxic gas since this is Astarte we're talking about! It goes into the atmosphere, or into the earth. It just drains away, back into the universe. It can't 'go' anywhere unless it's sent by the de-magicker. And you didn't send it anywhere, Tanz, so it just got reabsorbed.'

'Right. That's one theory up the spout. I've only got

one left, so I hope this one works. Gwydion was turned into a cat, because of some little prank on Merlin, right?'

Nest, Flissy and T.A. nodded.

'And he was my cat, right?'

They bobbed again, like a row of nodding dogs.

'Well, suppose that Astarte's magpie was someone who had been turned into a magpie by a magician as powerful as Merlin. When I turned Astarte into a frog, we all forgot about the magpie, right?'

Nod, nod, nod.

'Well, suppose the magpie flew back to wherever it came from, and suppose the magician forgave it, and suppose –'

'The magpie was actually Maebh all along, and now –' breathed Flissy.

'And now she is here, both Maebh and Astarte's magpie. And since Gwydion is, and probably always will be, a more powerful magician than me, then maybe what we have is someone even worse than Astarte Perkins and her horrible great-great-great-granny to worry about.'

T.A. shivered. 'Oh, don't, Tanz!'

'We have to, T.A.,' I said gently. 'We have to think the worst, because whoever has taken Gwydion and put him somewhere we can't reach him, has to be powerful. We mustn't ever underestimate the bad guys.'

'Tansy's right,' Aunty Fliss said slowly. 'Nest, do you agree? I mean, it sounds as if it could be right, but – who else is there? The Perkinses were nobodies, really. Astarte called up her big gun in *Merch Corryn*

55

Du but we dealt with her once and for all. Surely there isn't anyone else?'

'But look at all the evidence, Flissy!' I argued. 'Rhiryd ap Rhiryd Goch is back, and you said he has twin brothers as well. And there's Horrible Henbane, Maebh's right-hand slug.'

'Henbane?' Aunty Fliss said, 'who is he? If Maebh's the magpie, I mean.'

'He's the one who sort of recruited Iestyn – and they seem to think that by getting Iestyn in their clutches they will rule all the villagers. He's a poisonous little creep, that Henbane.'

'Well named, then,' put in Nest.

'Henbane? Why?'

'Well, if you look in my herbal, it describes the plant henbane as stickily hairy and foul-smelling. It is also extremely poisonous, and grows in disturbed ground. Which Ynys Haf certainly is at the moment!'

'Ha! Puts Master Henbane in a whole new light, doesn't it? But I don't think he's the powerful one, although I can't be entirely certain. He lets Maebh boss him about, but somehow I don't think her heart is in it. Between you and me, I think she's more scared of him than he is of her. However, we know Maebh can shape-shift – at least into one shape if not others. Who is she? Where does she come from? If we can find that out, at least it gives us a place to start.'

Fliss put her head in her hands. 'Oh, why isn't Merlin here? He's been around so long he's known all the family trees since they were acorns. But the wretch has gone off with Taliesin and they've turned off their auras, so we can't get at them.'

'Turned off their what-ahs?' I said, somewhat boggled.

'Auras. It's what makes a magician a magician,' Aunty Fliss explained. 'They give off a sort of magnetic force-field, so that other magicians – and witches, of course – can detect them wherever they are in the world. You have one, I have one. Even humans have them, although most of them don't know it and wouldn't recognise an aura if it stood up on its hind legs and waved at them. But powerful magicians can hide theirs. And they do, especially when they've gone off on a trip with another magician on a sort of big boys' jollyday. It looks as if they've turned off their auras so they can enjoy themselves in peace.'

'A bit like a mobile phone,' T.A. contributed helpfully.

'Mmm.'

'Which is why,' I said thoughtfully, 'Maebh was able to detect my presence even though I was only a ladybird. I'm going to have to learn how to turn mine off, right?'

'It might be a good idea. It's quite easy. You just visualise your magical aura – yours is somewhere between green and blue, by the way, and stretches all round your head and body. It's about half a metre wide, all round. First you imagine it – and then you imagine it gone.'

'Just like that,' I said. I tried to visualise a wide bluey, greeny aura. I thought I had it, but then it disappeared. 'I think I need some practice.'

'It will come, given time,' Nest said soothingly.

'We may not have time. Oh, who on earth can

57

Maebh be?' Aunty Fliss was looking more and more worried. 'She must be in the family tree somewhere. And at the back of my mind I have a feeling I know the branch. But I just can't remember it.'

'Tell you what, put it out of your mind and concentrate on something else for a while. It's a bit like trying to remember the title of a film or a song, or the name of an actor. The more you worry at it, the less likely you are to remember. And then, just as you are thinking something quite different, it pops into your head like –'

'Magic!' they all said together, and I laughed.

So, T.A. went back to her milking, I went to thank the bees for saving me from the magpie's beak, Nest decided to tidy her herbal medicines, and Flissy started on a pile of mending. When I came back she was mending a huge hole in a brown woolly sock.

'That Iestyn,' she said fondly. 'He goes through his socks like nobody's business. I'd say they were full of potatoes, except potatoes haven't been invented yet. And oh, Tansy, I have to say that once in a while, especially on a Sunday, I'd give my eye teeth for a nice, crispy roast spud!'

'With roast turkey and stuffing –'

'And brussels sprouts –'

'Ugh!'

'And garden peas, and gravy, and – I've got it!'

'Got what?'

'Great Aunt DisGrace!'

'Who?'

'Great Aunt DisGrace. She's related to Astarte and the Perkinses AND to us. She's a sort of second cousin

58

seven times removed from each side of each family – there was a witch and an Irish wizard in the – oh, must have been the third or fourth Ynys Haf century – who got entangled and got married. Jumped their broomsticks, which is what witches and wizards did in those days. Which is why the Emerald Spellorium and the Grimoire turned out to be such a problem to our family. It was all to do with inheritance. Centuries later, DisGrace's great-great-grandfather made a very muddly sort of will, and the Perkins decided they should have the Grimoire AND the Spellorium but of course we couldn't allow that, and that's how all the trouble started.'

I didn't need reminding of the trouble the Grimoire caused. Retrieving that bad spell book and putting it out of harm's way had been my first daunting task as a witch!

'Anyway,' continued Fliss 'the marriage might all have turned out for the best, uniting the two families, except that this witch and this wizard had one nice child and one thoroughly nasty one. We are descended from the nice one, and Great Aunt DisGrace is descended from the nasty one, and I'll bet Maebh is descended from her. Or maybe she even *is* her. I met her once, years ago, at a friend's baby's christening in Our Time.'

'What on earth was a witch doing at a christening, Fliss?'

'Oh, come on, Tansy! There are always witches – and fairies, sometimes – at christenings. Who do you think gives them their life-gifts? *Sleeping Beauty* and so on?'

'Oh, Aunty Fliss. You're winding me up now, right?'

She looked amazed. 'Of course I'm not!'

She wasn't, of course. Even though I'd been a witch for a fair while now, every now and again my human culture came up against my witch culture with a great, big clang . . .

Nest, hearing our discussion, had abandoned her spring-cleaning and was listening.

'So, if Maebh is related to this Great Aunt DisGrace,' I said, 'or even *is* Great Aunt DisGrace, what does that tell us?'

'Well, we now have a place to look for Gwydion.'

'We do?'

'Of course.'

'Where?'

Flissy gazed at me, fondness mingled with exasperation in her expression. 'Well, Ireland, of course. Where else? Where did Maebh come from? And Henbane?'

'Ireland.'

'And where people come from, they leave traces. That's where we can learn more about them.'

'So,' I snorted, 'we only have to search the whole of Ireland for Maebh's footmarks, leading to an enchanted Gwydion!'

'We can make a start. It's worth a try,' said Fliss firmly.

'I have cousins in the Land of Finn MacCuill,' Nest put in. 'There's Boylan, and Regan, and O'Liam of the Green Boots, he's my favourite.'

'Leprechauns, I suppose,' I said, jokingly.

'What else?' Nest smiled, happily. 'Oh, it's ages since I've seen them, hundreds and hundreds of years, and it would do my heart good to see my family again.'

My brain was still trying to take in leprechauns in the family. Why not, though? There were witches, wizards, and Nest was half *tylwyth teg*. Why should I have trouble believing in leprechauns?

'Are they green?' I just had to ask, didn't I?

Nest laughed. 'Of course not! That's just a silly story put about by humans. They're exactly the same colour as we are, but shinier. A wee bit smaller than us, agreed, but the same colour. They do tend to be red-haired rather a lot, and they can be a bit on the mischievous side.' (She wasn't suggesting a likeness, was she? I'm sensitive about my colouring.)

'Their main fault is they can't help being sneaky. It's in the blood, you see,' Nest went on fondly. 'Oh, my cousin Boylan once did something remarkable with a pot of gold and a rainbow – it had people digging up fields for centuries, after.'

'Can we scry Ireland? Maybe we can find Gwydion that way.'

'We could,' Aunt Fliss said thoughtfully, 'but it would be better if you went there. You need to take Nest, I think, since she is related to the Little People. Maybe they will help you.'

'When should we go?' I asked, facing up to the inevitable.

'As soon as you can, I think, Tansy. Iestyn will be here to keep an eye on Maebh. We will get word to you somehow if anything urgent comes up. Go tomorrow.'

T.A. had finished the milking and had been listening very hard for the past ten minutes. She made a sort of pleading squeak. I knew exactly what *that* meant.

'What do you think, Aunty Fliss? Should I take T.A. or not?'

Aunty Fliss considered. 'I don't see why not. She is a sensible girl, and she might help keep you out of trouble.'

T.A. stuck her tongue out at me behind Aunty Fliss's back, and I pulled a face.

'Her, sensible? In a parallel universe.'

'Which is exactly where we are,' T.A. said. 'That's settled, then. I'm coming. How shall we travel, Aunty Fliss? Seagulls?'

Nest shook her head. 'Absolutely not. Neither of you have shape-shifted for that distance. Your wings wouldn't be nearly strong enough to take you across the sea. You'd be blown half to Atlantis and back and get nowhere near Ireland. No, we shall go by boat.'

I swallowed. I am a very, very bad sailor. I get seasick on ponds, right? I was *not* looking forward to a sea-crossing. But hey. I'd never done a ferry crossing as a witch before. Maybe witches don't get sea sick . . .

7

All together now – *oh yes they do!*

But that came later. First we had to find a boat that was willing to take us over to Ireland.

Just to prove how totally dumb I can be, I was sort of expecting to arrive at, say, Fishguard, hop on a nice big passenger ferry or a tidy little seacat, whiz across the Irish Sea, hop off at Rosslare, and say hello to Ireland. I mean, *twp* or what?

For a start, we flew to the coast, but the coast wasn't where it should have been. The great cities of the western lowlands, Cantre'r Gwaelod, were still above the sea, still ruled by King Gwyddno Garanhir, whom I had met at Gwydion's Kingmaking, and we would be putting out from somewhere along that coast, where Aberdyfi would one day be, only wasn't yet, if you see what I mean.

The three of us shape-shifted into gulls and took off from the *tŷ hir*, soaring up into a blue spring sky with only a trace of wind. It took us a long time to reach Cantre'r Gwaelod, because we had to make frequent stops for T.A. and me to rest our aching wings. Nest was absolutely right, we were in no shape to make the crossing under our own steam.

Towards sunset, we circled low over the tall towers of the sixteen cities of Cantre'r Gwaelod, and swooped down to land in the courtyard of the King's palace. It was wonderful countryside: lush grass and clear rivers shaded by dark trees; herds of deer; lakes; you name it, Cantre'r Gwaelod had it. It also had the towering sea-wall and the huge sluice gate that kept the incoming tide out of Cantre'r Gwaelod. The trouble was, of course, that I knew the legend – that one day the sluice-gate keeper (Seithennyn, that was his name) would get mightily ratted on something alcoholic, pass out and forget to close the sluice-gates before the tide turned. And everyone in the sixteen cities – except Taliesin, who would be there as Gwyddno Garanhir's bard and magician – would drown. The awful thing was, I couldn't warn them. Wasn't allowed, apparently. That would change history, and interfere with the natural balance of Ynys Haf and, and, and. Taliesin had explained it all at great length. Oh, and threatened me. I think he said he'd turn me into a bluebottle and swat me. Anyway, I got the message.

So I had to go through the greeting bit, and the politeness bit, and the supper bit, all the time hoping that this wasn't the night of the Big Flood. Then I remembered that since Taliesin wasn't around, it couldn't be, since it would be changing history if it happened when he was elsewhere, so I relaxed a bit.

He was a nice old boy, Gwyddno, and made us very welcome. We had a big banquet and lots and lots and lots of toasts, and T.A. got a little bit rat-faced on mead and started flirting with Elffin, with whom she had got on rather well last time they'd met. I had to drag her off to our chamber and put her to bed. She giggled a lot before she went to sleep.

Next morning we had to wait for the tide, and so Elffin took T.A. and me on a sort of V.I.P. inspection of the sea wall. It was a pretty impressive piece of engineering, I'll say that for it. The tide was turning, and the gate-keeper was turning the great wheel which hauled the sluice-gates shut against the incoming waves. I gazed down from the sea-wall onto the top of his bald head and was tempted to *order* him to quit drinking on pain of being turned into a toad, but that would have been cheating too, I expect. I contented myself with saying darkly and mysteriously (well, I am a witch, after all!) to Elffin, 'Watch that fellow, Elffin. Something about him smells untrustworthy.'

Elffin grinned, and his dimples danced. 'That would be his stockings, Lady Tan'ith. Mind you, he changes them once a year whether he needs to or not.'

What's the use, eh? At least I tried.

'Ah!' Elffin shaded his eyes and peered out to sea. There's your boat coming in on the tide.'

I peered in the general direction of out-to-sea, but couldn't see anything. 'Our boat? Where?'

'There,' Elffin flung out an arm and I followed his pointing finger. Far out I saw a tiny – an extremely tiny – black dot. The trouble was, it didn't get much bigger when it got closer.

'That's not a boat!' I said as it pulled alongside the sea wall, 'that's a walnut shell.'

Perhaps I was exaggerating a bit, but it wasn't much bigger. It was about as long as a small bus, with an arched prow at one end and a high sort of platform thingy at the back. In the middle was a hut with open sides. A large, square sail was currently being reefed, or folded, or whatever sailors call taking down a sail so your ship won't blow away. It looked more than anything like a Viking longship, only this was a shortship, if you get my drift. And I was going to get on that and cross all that sea to Ireland? No way, chum.

On the other hand, maybe I was. Aunt Nest appeared at my elbow, laden down with warm sheepskins. I'd have preferred a lifebelt, personally. 'Put these on, Tansy, T.A.,' she said, handing us one each. 'The wind is getting up and it will be cold out there.'

'Nest,' I said, carefully, trying not to shriek, 'are you quite sure we aren't strong enough to fly? We had lots of practice yesterday, after all.'

'And how do your arms feel?' she enquired.

I lifted mine to shoulder height. I couldn't get them any higher. 'Fine,' I whimpered.

'Liar,' she said. 'Get on the boat.'

T.A., who must have Viking ancestry somewhere in her past, leapt lightly down the iron ladder on the sea-wall, hopped on board and shot up to the pointed end with a big grin on her face, Nest climbed down onto the deck and looked up at me. 'Come on, Tansy. The quicker you get on board, the quicker we'll be there. You'll be fine once we get going.'

All together again, folks. '*Oh no, she won't.*'

As soon as the grizzled looking chap with the tarry pigtail cast off the ropes for'ard and aft (or whatever) and the boat turned its nose to the open sea, I felt my breakfast start its journey upward . . .

Shouting at the seashells, technicolour yawns, upchucking, painting the porcelain, barfing, whatever you care to call it, I did it. Half way across the Irish Sea I was afraid I was going to die. Three-quarters of

66

the way across I was afraid I might live to carry on feeling as awful as I did right then.

And all the time Nest patted my back and held my head and scooped my hair back off my face every time I sagged over the side to throw up.

The four sailors were highly amused, and yelled merry quips like 'Get it up, young 'un! Do yer good!', and 'How about a nice bit of fatty bacon, m'dear?', and 'Lovely shade of green on 'er!'. If I hadn't been feeling so utterly deathly I might possibly have turned the whole lot of them into jellyfish, or rats, or sea-cucumbers, see if they could still make jokes when they were flopping about on the bottom of the boat.

At last, however, I raised my whirling head and saw a greenness ahead of the boat. Naturally, because the boat was going uuuuup and doooown, uuuuup and doooown, it looked as if the land was doing the same thing, but then I realised it wasn't, and fixed my eyes on the horizon as if it was the Promised Land ahead of me. I hoped it was actually Ireland. It seemed to me as if we'd been at sea long enough to get to America. And back.

But then we sailed inside a sea wall, the waves dropped, the wind died away, and the sun shone through rainclouds. A rainbow framed the greenness that was Ireland and I began to feel Much Better.

I felt better still (although the ground persisted in going up and down) after I was off the boat.

'Nest,' I said, weakly. 'I hope you aren't planning on going anywhere right at this minute. I think I need to rest a while before we start looking for whatever we're looking for.' Well, I knew what I meant.

'You need something to eat,' she said, patting me. 'You're stomach is hollow as a drum.'

'No kidding,' I moaned.

They helped me totter up the little path from the jetty. Half way up the hill was a small, whitewashed cottage set into the hillside. It had an altogether crazy roof. I had to look twice to make sure I wasn't imagining things. It was a sort of rounded mound, and it was covered in grass and flowers all growing wildly and waving in the breeze. Two goats and a brown cow were tethered on it, peacefully munching grass, and they looked up curiously as we passed. Smoke drifted from a hole in the top of the mound, and the sound of someone singing – badly – drifted through the open door.

Nest rapped on the door-frame and stuck her head through the doorway.

'Peace be on all who dwell here,' she said, and the singing stopped.

'And peace be upon you what visits,' replied a deep voice from within. 'Can I help you at all?'

'A meal, if you have food to spare,' Nest asked politely. 'We will gladly pay.'

'Food I have, and have it you shall,' came the voice again. 'Pay you shall not, for the day when a hungry traveller passes my door without welcome is the day I shall die.'

What was weird about this exchange was that, although the words sounded friendly, the tone of voice didn't. Its owner appeared in the doorway, and stared at us suspiciously through narrow, yellowish eyes. She was big, but not fat. She had huge muscles and wide

68

shoulders which went oddly with the neat grey dress and sacking apron she wore. She actually rather resembled an all-in wrestler. But she ushered us inside and sat us at a table very like the one we had left behind in the *tŷ hir*.

'I have fish in plenty, and soda bread,' she offered, 'and milk from my beasts.'

'We are grateful for your food and the welcome from your heart,' Nest said, and she, too, sounded as if she were reciting lines someone else had written for her.

Personally, I had the feeling that fish might prove the last straw, but when I smelled it cooking, and tasted it, sweet and fresh from the sea, the silvery creature disappeared down my throat rather faster than polite manners would allow. Mam would have rapped my knuckles with a spoon and told me not to gobble. When I'd finished, and even managed to get some creamy, strong-tasting milk down my throat, I was as full as an egg.

I gazed at the strong woman gratefully. 'I can't thank you enough,' I said. 'Honestly, you saved my life. Anything I –' I was startled to find my shins kicked, hard, by Nest.

The woman stared at me, but spoke to Nest. 'The young one should take care what she says, stranger. To owe someone a life is a powerful thing in this part of the world.'

'Indeed it is,' Nest replied, humbly. 'But the young one comes from a far off land. She does not understand. Forgive her, if you will, and be charitable.'

The woman scowled at me. ''Twould be my right

should I care to take it,' she said at last. 'But since she is a stranger to this land, then I will forgive the debt this once.'

'For your good kindness, let us leave an unworthy gift for your winter's winter?'

I didn't have a clue what they were on about, so I just kept quiet. T.A. was looking from me, to Nest, to the woman, with an expression rather like panic on her face.

'A gift for my winter's winter, then. And then you go and do not come back.'

Nest handed over a few coins, and we gathered up our sheepskin jerkins and left. Nest ushered me out of the door first, T.A. second, and last of all, came through herself.

Just as I went through the low door the strange, big-boned woman said loudly, 'Witch?'

I almost turned, and then, somehow, I don't know how or why, I managed to resist it.

We got to the brow of the hill, and as soon as we were over it and out of sight of the woman and her cottage, Nest sank down on the harsh sea-grass.

'Oh, Tan'ith! Whatever it was that made you not turn when she called you witch, I am grateful for it. If you had turned we should have been lost.'

'What? Nest, I am thoroughly confused.'

Nest put her head in her hands. 'Oh, I should have known. I hadn't expected the Sea-Guardian to be a woman, that's all.'

'Still confused, Nest.'

'We were lucky to get out of there at all, Tan'ith!'

'Extremely, very confused, Nest.'

The half-fairy took a deep breath, brushing her dark, glossy hair behind her ears. 'How can I explain? Well, you know that in your time you have people guarding the ports to make sure that travellers are who they say they are and not smugglers, or bad people?'

'Customs and Excise?' I stared at her. 'Are you telling me that tough old bird is a *customs officer?*'

'Sort of. She's there to make sure that nothing threatening comes in through the port. She can sniff out witches and fairies and wizards like a bloodhound.'

'She can? Then how come she didn't sniff us out?'

'Because I switched off our auras, Tansy, yours and mine. But then you almost started talking about her saving your life, which here has much more than the careless throwaway meaning you give it in your Time.'

'Much more how?' I was feeling distinctly unsteady.

'If someone saves your life, then they own it. And to own a witch's life is to own her powers. Which is why she called out "witch" as we left. A tiny inkling of your aura must have crept back, and she sniffed it out. If you had turned, she would have had you. And your magic.'

'Oh, shoot.'

'I second that,' T.A.'s voice was definitely shaky. 'Nest, don't you think we ought to find somewhere we can hide while you sort of bring us up to date on any other little problems we might run into in Ireland?'

71

8

So we shape-shifted into sparrows and flew around a
bit until we found a cave we could hide in overnight.
There didn't seem to be much in the way of houses or
people around, so it seemed safe enough to light a fire
just inside the entrance. The cave was half-way up a
mountain, and when we had shifted back from
sparrows I peered inside nervously. 'I hope there
aren't any snakes in there. Or wolves, or bears.
Anything else in the wildlife line I should know about,
Nest?'

'There certainly aren't wolves or bears: you'd smell
them in the cave if there were, and there'd be bones
and other left-over bits lying about. And St Patrick got
rid of the snakes in Ireland ages ago, so don't worry
about that, either. No, we'll be perfectly safe here. The
cave roof isn't high enough for a giant.'

I chuckled. 'Giants . . .' Then I realised Nest was
Looking at me. 'Oh, no. Are you trying to tell me
that Ireland has giants? Come on, Nest, they're
nothing but a –'

'Fairy story? Like witches and wizards?' Nest was
smiling. 'Listen, Tansy. While you are here, expect the
unexpected. Don't take anything in Ireland at its face
value and you'll possibly get out of here in one piece.'

'Is Ireland that dangerous, then?' I think T.A. was
beginning to wish she hadn't come.

'No more dangerous than Ynys Haf. But just as you
have to take care in Ynys Haf, so you have to take care

here. More so, because the Irish have different customs. So it would be a good idea, Lady,' she said softly, looking at me, 'if you let me do the talking wherever possible. Once I have met up with my cousins we shall be safer, but there is a ritual to that, just as there was with the Guardian, and I must get it right first time or we shall get nowhere. Leprechauns are great ones for sending people in circles.'

'So, you were joking about giants, then?'

Nest shook her head. 'Of course not. Mind, Ireland is the last place you will find them, although there was a tale a while ago that some place in the Lands of Ice and Snow had trolls that were almost as large. There aren't many left – most of them have died out, but a few may be hibernating. So we must keep our eyes open all the time. For instance, if this cave had long strands of what looked like rope dangling from the roof, I wouldn't have let you come in here. And we certainly should not have lit a fire the way we did.'

I had to ask, didn't I? 'Why?'

'Because very probably you would have been camping up a giant's nose. And no one in their right mind lights a fire up a giant's nose.'

I gulped. 'And the ropes?'

'The hairs in his nose, of course. But don't worry. While I am with you, I'll make sure you don't trip over any bits of giant.'

Don't worry! Was she kidding, or what?

'So,' Nest went on. 'It's agreed. I do the talking, you do the listening and keep your eyes and ears open, right?'

'Right,' T.A. and I agreed fervently.

Surprisingly, I fell asleep quite quickly. I suppose throwing up all day had tired me out.

During the night I sort of half-woke, but went straight back to sleep again. And yet, when I woke up the next morning, I had this vague memory of the cave being filled with golden light . . . Not the sun, not daylight at all. A goldness had glinted off the rocky roof and walls and made me feel warm and safe.

I felt rather less warm and safe in the morning. I felt thoroughly hungry, and a bit chilly despite the sunshine coming in at the cave's mouth.

'Hungry?' Nest asked.

I nodded. 'As a hunter.'

'Then hunters we shall be,' Nest said, and shape-shifted into a fox. I quickly shifted T.A. and then myself into similar lithe red creatures and together we loped out of the cave. Half way down the hillside we spotted a small group of rabbits and suddenly I wished I had shifted into a bird, instead. I could eat nuts and berries, no problem, but being in a fox-pelt meant crunching up a bunny, and crunching up a bunny was altogether too – delicious. Yum. I sat back on my haunches and licked my furry chops. It's amazing what a good appetite and a shape-shift will do for a girl. When we returned to the cave and shifted back, however, I noticed that T.A. was looking a bit green around the gills.

'What's up, T.A.?' I asked, knowing perfectly well what.

'We murdered those rabbits!' she whispered, and put her hand over her mouth.

'We had to eat,' Nest said sternly, overhearing her, 'and rabbits are good for foxes.'

74

'But I'm not a –'

'When you are in another creature's skin, you must feed that creature what it usually eats,' I said firmly. 'Otherwise you will make it ill. Just be grateful we didn't shift into moles, T.A. They eat –'

'I know, I know. Just shut up, Tanz, OK?'

'When you two have quite finished, I think we should start to move away from here. If the Guardian of the Port is still suspicious, she may be following us. I think we threw her off the scent, but when we shape-shift, we are off guard, and she may sense us then.'

'So, shall we walk or fly?'

'I think we should fly. If we go quickly, then we shall get well ahead of her and we can forget her. Until we need to go back to Ynys Haf, that is.'

'There is no way, Nest,' I said firmly, 'that I am going to get back on *anything* that floats ever again.'

'If you say so, Tan'ith,' Nest said, demurely. I looked at her suspiciously, but her expression gave nothing away.

'We don't want to be anything that can get hunted, right?' T.A. said nervously. 'Can we be something fast, and something that hunts, instead?'

'Kestrels?' I suggested, and Nest nodded.

I shifted T.A., and then Nest and I shimmered, shifted, stretched reluctant arms into delicate wing bones, pushed pin- and tail-feathers out of pink skins, and the three of us stood, sturdy birds with reddish backs and dark blue heads, stretching our wings and sensing the wind's lift. And then we leapt into the air and flew inland, powerful wing-beats driving us onward.

75

The land below us undulated, and I began to see why Ireland is said to have forty shades of green. We flew over soft green slopes, and dark green trees, and emerald green meadows, and craggy outcrops with tufts of sage green sticking out like hair on a balding head. My kestrel eyesight picked out the swift freezing of a vole as we flew overhead, lying low, like Brer Rabbit, and saying nuffin'. Luckily for it, I wasn't feeling hungry.

We had flown for about an hour, and my wings were beginning to ache when Nest began to circle and descend over a dark mass of tree-tops. We landed in one of them and perched next to each other.

'This looks familiar. I think my cousins live somewhere near here,' Nest squawked. 'Come on.'

Obediently, T.A. and I followed her, swooping down through the heavy branches until we landed in a clearing. Nest and I shimmered, and then I changed T.A. back. T.A. was standing with her arms outspread and her eyes closed.

'Every time you shift me, it feels sort of fizzy in my bones,' she said. 'It's like trying to put on a really tight pair of rubber washing-up gloves. You have to sort of squish bits of you into the right shape to make it all fit properly.'

'Exactly,' I agreed. 'But isn't it nice when everything goes back in the right place?'

T.A. shuddered. 'Ooh, don't, Tanz! What if –'

'Don't even think about it, that's my advice,' I said, laughing. 'Think positive.'

'When you two are quite ready,' Nest said, reprovingly, 'I think we need to look around, see what we can see.'

'OK,' we said in unison. Then 'Um. What are we looking for, exactly?' I asked.

'Little People,' Nest said. 'You'll know them if you see them. I know they are round here somewhere. They might even be watching us right now. We won't see them until they want us to.'

'What if they don't?' I muttered. 'Could be a long day, Nest.'

'Of course they will,' she retorted. 'They're *family*!'

We spread out across the clearing and began to look. I still didn't have the faintest idea what we were looking for, and then, after a while, T.A. squeaked excitedly.

I sprinted over to her. She was pointing at something in the grass. 'Look!' she breathed.

It was a boot, with a long curved toe, high tops cut in points, made of emerald leather. And it was barely six inches long. Nest peered over our shoulders. 'Ah!' she said. 'Just what I was hoping for. It's him.'

'You may not have noticed, Nest,' I pointed out, 'but there's only one boot, and there isn't anyone in it.'

'Exactly,' she replied. 'There's only one person I know who wears boots like that, and he's always in a state of mad panic. When he heard us coming he'd have leapt out of here so fast he left his boot behind. O'Liam, I know you're around somewhere. It's me, your cousin Nest. Come out, O'Liam of the Green Boots. No need to be afraid of us.'

For a while, nothing happened, and then I noticed a strange golden glow behind a tree, as if the sun were hiding behind it, and shining out both sides. I nudged Nest, whispering. 'Look. Over there.'

Nest clapped her hands. 'I see you, O'Liam! Please come out. My friends may be a bit on the big side, but they're quite friendly.'

Slowly, a nose edged out from behind the tree, followed by a small face. He was smaller than Nest, barely three feet high, with a sharp little face seemingly made up entirely of angles and points, like a dog-fox. He wasn't green, but he was entirely glowing, as if he had a candle inside him. I suddenly remembered the golden glow in the cave when I had half-woken the night before, and began to suspect that O'Liam – or someone like him – had been watching us all along.

O'Liam edged sideways, collected his boot and replaced it on his foot, which wore a violently coloured striped sock with holes in heel and toe.

'Is it yourself, Nest?' he asked. 'Or is it someone else entirely, pretending to be you?'

'It's me, O'Liam. Oh, there's lovely to see you.' And Nest stepped forward, her arms outstretched, preparing to give him a hug.

'Ah, none of your hugs and kisses, woman,' he said, backing away. 'I don't go for that sort of thing at all. Not on a Wednesday, anyhow. Try me tomorrow.'

T.A. put her hand over her mouth, and stifled a snort. I glared at her. She mustn't offend him.

He cocked his head at her, his bright eyes sharp. 'And who might the dark beauty be, Nest?' he asked. 'The one with the fine sense of humour there.'

'This is T.A.,' Nest said. 'She's mortal, but special.'

'Will I like her?' he asked.

'You will indeed,' Nest replied. It was almost like a strange ritual.

'And who might the rare one with the hair on her like a sunset be? And the fine Irish freckles also?'

Now I quite liked that. Better than Sion ap Sion's spotty dapples. Hair like a sunset? I could live with that. I opened my mouth and then remembered Nest's warning and shut it again.

'This,' Nest said softly, 'is the Lady.'

'The Lady? Is she so? She's terrible, awful young to be the Lady.'

'She is the strongest of all the witches of Ynys Haf, and young she may be, O'Liam of the Green Boots, but the Lady has given her all her powers and one day she will rule Ynys Haf beside Gwydion Dragonking.'

'Ah yes. I had heard that the Dragonson was the Dragonking. I welcome you, Lady,' the little man said, bowing over his green boots. 'I think you'd best come with me, cousin Nest. And mind the brambles there. You know what they say – less haste, more weed.'

And he opened a door in a very large oak and disappeared inside it.

9

OK. Before I tell you what it was like inside the tree, I want you to forget you ever saw anything by Walt Disney, and anything with Little People in it, right? Right.

We followed O'Liam of the Green Boots down a steep spiral staircase, roots of plants and trees dangling all round us. We ran as fast as we could to keep up with his twinkling feet. The fact that he glowed golden was a great help, so long as we could keep him in sight around the twisting staircase. He was like a torch, travelling at 100 miles an hour!

At the bottom he opened a wooden door and darted through it, leaving it open for us to follow.

I suppose I expected loads and loads of Leprechauns (yes, green ones, I admit it) jigging around to bodhrans and Irish bagpipes and penny whistles, clicking their heels and saying 'Ah, begorrah!' and twinkling a lot in a thoroughly Oirish way. Wrong.

We were in a huge cavern, blazing with light that reflected from raw crystals set in the walls. The place was possibly the busiest place I've ever seen. Everywhere golden glowing figures were bent over desks, or standing round talking softly in sober, important-looking groups. At the far end of the chamber was a huge polished wooden table, and seated around it were twelve of the oldest people I think I've ever seen. Oh, and one young one.

'I'll tell the Council you're come,' O'Liam whispered, and shot off towards them.

Actually, he didn't 'shoot' so much as flicker: when the small people moved, they did it without actually seeming to do so. One minute they were in one place, then there was a blurring of the air, and then they suddenly appeared in another place altogether, without any effort at all. It was a bit like freeze-frame photography, and unnerving to watch. I almost expected 'Phhhht!' sound-effects, but it was totally silent.

O'Liam appeared beside the young man seated at the big table, and waited politely, his hat twisting in his hands rather like Iestyn twisted his when he was around important people. The young man finished what he was saying and turned to O'Liam, his golden head on one side. O'Liam bent and whispered in his ear, and the young man's eyes flickered towards us, the way a snake's tongue flickers in-and-out when it's testing the air: and then he was beckoning us forward.

'Remember,' Nest muttered. 'I do the talking, Tan'ith – promise?'

I didn't need any reminding. 'Promise,' I said. I clamped my lips shut and walked forward behind Nest, trying very hard to look dignified. If I had been wearing something long and sweeping and Ladylike, I might have managed it, but salt-and-sick-stained breeches and sheepskin jerkin didn't quite do it. Maybe we should have magicked something better, but I hadn't even thought of it. I tried telling myself that real dignity came from the soul, and clothes didn't matter, but didn't manage to convince myself.

The radiant young man was very handsome, with the same sharp features that O'Liam had, although he looked more wolfish than foxy and was taller, close to four feet, which must have been tall for a leprechaun. Below a golden circlet his eyes were huge and golden, and rimmed with dark lashes, and he studied us carefully as we approached.

'Conor of the Land Beneath, I bring you greetings from the *Tylwyth Teg*,' Nest began, 'and from your cousins in Ynys Haf who love and remember you with honour. Please forgive that we visit without invitation or permission, but we have great difficulty in Ynys Haf, and we need your help if you should graciously decide to give it.'

'Welcome to you, Nest, without invitation or permission.' I think he was smiling, but maybe it was just his lips twitching. For such a handsome creature, it was strange that he gave off such a feeling of coldness.

'Is your Dragonson not become Dragonking, then, as We had heard?'

'He has, Lord Conor. But he has disappeared, and we believe he has been stricken by a sleeping glamour.'

Glamour? What was she on about? Then I remembered that 'glamour' was an olde worde for 'spell'.

'Has he so? And who would do such a thing to a Dragonking crowned?'

'Ah, my Lord Conor. That is where we hope you can help us.'

Lord Conor raised a dark eyebrow, quizzically, then

82

waved an arm at the circle of grey-beards-down-to-their-knees crumblies sitting around the table. 'My wise companions, forgive me. I have family matters to consider.'

I was rather glad he wasn't *my* family.

The old men got creakily to their feet and tottered away, each clutching a pile of parchment rolls. Some of them had quill pens stuck behind their ears, which made them look like rather odd birds.

Conor of the Land Beneath waved his arm, inviting us to sit at his table. 'Will you not introduce me to your companions, Nest? His eyes flickered over us.

'With pleasure, and I am honoured to do so, Lord Conor of the Land Beneath. This is the Lady Tan'ith. Although she is young, she is a Daughter of the Moon, and is now the Lady of Ynys Haf and Custodian of the Magical Island. The other is known as Haf, and is her trusted friend and companion.'

Lord Conor inspected us without speaking. After a while it got uncomfortable, and made me want to wriggle, but I sat as still as I could, my back straight, trying very hard to meet those glittering golden eyes without blinking.

'This one is the Lady, to be sure,' he said at last. 'For despite her stained clothing she has the Look. But the other one is different. She is mortal, is she not?'

T.A. went pale. I think she was trying to remember fairy tales about leprechauns' attitudes to mortals.

'She is, Lord Conor,' Nest agreed, smiling. 'Both the Lady and Haf have lived their lives in the Aboveworld, but they have both risked crossing in Time because we needed them.'

'Can the mortal be trusted?'

'With our lives, Lord Conor.'

'With yours, perhaps,' Conor said. 'But I am King and Lord of the Land Beneath, and I do not trust so easily. And so. How might one so humble as I help the Lady of Ynys Haf?'

Ha! I thought, Conor, humble? No way.

Nest turned to me and nodded, and I realised that now I was allowed to speak. The expression on her face told me to be extremely careful of what I said. And how I said it.

'Lord Conor of the Land Beneath,' I began formally, 'as Lady Nest has told you, Gwydion Dragonking has disappeared. We have scryed him, and found him in an enchanted sleep. He is alive, but we do not know where he is, or who has cast the spell.' All this posh sort of talk was a bit wearing, but I persevered. If Nest thought it was necessary to talk like that, it was good enough for me. 'After he was enchanted,' I went on, 'a woman claiming to be of royal blood came to Ynys Haf, and has installed herself in Castell Du, together with her retainers. She is from your country, and we hope that you can help us find out who she is and where she has come from. Once we know this, perhaps we can find Gwydion Dragonking and restore him to his senses and his kingdom.' Well, I thought it sounded good. Nest nodded slightly: I'd done OK.

Conor steepled his fingers and pursed his lips. The great golden eyes half closed, and his glow grew slightly brighter. Maybe he was thinking. The silence stretched for ages. Then, abruptly, he stood up.

'I shall consider it. In the meantime, you shall refresh yourselves and join me at supper.' He snapped his fingers and half a dozen glowing girls appeared, each demurely smiling, and led us away to a room with three bath tubs filled with steaming milky water on which strawberry leaves floated. It didn't take much encouragement for us to leap in and scrub ourselves all over.

I'm not very tall, five-feet-two if I breathe in and stand tall, but honestly, I felt positively gigantic beside the leprechaun girls! Even Nest looked a bit on the lofty side. And yet, when they brought us a variety of silken gowns to wear, *they all fitted.* Go figure, if you'll pardon the pun. Then I remembered they were leprechauns, and probably had a fair bit of casual magic at their glowing fingertips.

So we three got poshed up, and admired each others' dresses, and let the girls brush our hair and arrange it – they did mine in rather fetching French plaits – and were ready for dinner when the trumpet sounded. Actually, I was ready long before – it had been a long time since my breakfast bunny. We followed the girls down a corridor towards a wonderful smell of food. At the doorway Nest stood back and nodded for me to go ahead of her, so I put my nose in the air and swept grandly into a great hall with a huge table laid for supper.

Lord Conor, beautifully dressed in dark ruby velvet, bowed over my hand and escorted me to a seat beside him. Nest went to his left, and T.A. on the other side of me on his right. I was so hungry I had to try very hard not to gobble, but the food was so delicious. The wine was wonderful too, but I drank very little. I had a feeling I would need all my senses as sharp as possible. I probably ate too much, but afterwards, I felt a whole lot happier.

When we had eaten, a girl with a small harp and a beautiful voice sang to us, and there was a bit of expert and intricate dancing (to watch, not to join in, which I was glad about. I was so full!), and then the evening was finished. Conor (who had been frighteningly charming the socks off me all evening) kissed my hand and wished me good night.

'We shall talk tomorrow, Lady. Sleep well.' He was handsome, I have to admit. If only he'd been about a two feet taller and hadn't reminded me quite so much of a small, beautiful, deadly snake . . .

Besides, who could hold a candle to Gwydion? He was always in my mind. Even back in my time, whenever a boy asked me out, perhaps to the cinema or a disco, I'd go, but there was always a third person with us, invisible, but there. Didn't actually seem fair, when I thought about it. Not since he had obviously got close enough to that Maebh person for her to put a spell on him, the rat.

We slept in huge, silken-sheeted beds, in a row like the Three Bears, and were woken when a couple of golden girls pitched up with breakfast. Our clothes were returned, cleaned (thank goodness! Mine had been distinctly smelly) and we washed and dressed ready for our meeting with Conor.

'Do you think he'll help us, Nest?' I whispered, not sure who might be listening.

'I don't know. I hope so. But with leprechauns, you

never can tell. And he might want something in return, so be careful what you say. Any promise you make you must keep. So be aware and *beware*, the whole time.'

'Remember Rumpelstiltskin, Tanz,' T.A. said jokingly.

'Yes,' Nest said, 'remember Rumpelstiltskin.' But Nest wasn't joking.

I stared at her. 'What! First born child and all that? Oh, Nest, you're kidding.'

Nest shook her head. 'Just be careful, Tan'ith. Listen to the voice of Ynys Haf.'

'Bit far away for that, Nest.'

'Ynys Haf is inside you, Tan'ith. You are part of it as it is part of you. Listen to it, draw on it, use it. It will help you. When we meet Conor, you must do the talking. You are the Lady, and it is you who must explain and ask for help. All I can do now is sit and listen.'

Oh-oh. I got that 'who, me?' feeling again.

Soon after that O'Liam, his green boots twinkling, led us to Conor's chamber. A log fire burned at one end, and high-backed chairs were set round an intricately carved table with a huge round mirror set flat in the centre.

'Scrying mirror,' Nest muttered under her breath as we sat down. 'Keep your eye on it.'

The surface of the mirror seemed smoky, but strange things flickered in its depths, like trout in a deep pool.

'Did you sleep well, now?' Conor enquired politely.

'We did,' I answered, and T.A. and Nest agreed.

87

'Our grateful thanks to you for your hospitality, Lord Conor. We are honoured by your generosity.' I caught Nest's faint nod of approval.

'Now, Lady Tan'ith,' Conor began, sitting in his carved chair, 'tell me what has been happening in Ynys Haf. It is a fair long time since I was there: when your Gwydion Dragonson's father was crowned, I think. I was made most welcome.'

I stared at him. But that was centuries ago! He couldn't be more than thirty at the most – and then I remembered he was a leprechaun, and revised my opinion of Lord Conor. I should have to be very careful indeed.

'Gwydion Dragonson was crowned King in his turn,' I began, 'but not without a few problems –'

'Astarte Perkins and the Spiderwitch,' Conor said smoothly. '*Merch Corryn Du*, was that not the outlandish name the woman had?'

'You know?' I was startled.

'Of course. I make it my business to know what happens in Ynys Haf, just as I do in Cornwall, Man, the Out Isles, Brittany, and even the Lost Lands.'

'So,' I said, beginning to feel very wary. 'You knew about Gwydion before we got here.'

But he shook his head. 'No. For some reason the – em, *enquirer* that was sent to Ynys Haf has not yet returned.' He steepled his fingers again and gazed innocently into my eyes.

Enquirer? He meant spy. It had never crossed my mind that there would be spies in Ynys Haf.

Feeling my way very carefully, as if I were alone in a very dark, strange room, I said, 'Just before

Gwydion disappeared, an Irish girl arrived in Ynys Haf, claiming royal blood. We don't know why she came, or even how, but shortly after Gwydion disappeared she and her people moved into Castell Du and now she is calling herself Queen of Ynys Haf.'

'Is she so?' Conor picked up a goose-quill pen and pulled a sheet of parchment towards him. He dipped the quill into a big golden inkwell, poised it over the paper, but didn't write anything. 'And was your Dragonking taken with the girl?'

Nest spoke up. 'I believe he might have been, Lord Conor. She is very beautiful.'

'Hmm. And what would her name be, if you'll be so kind as to tell me?'

'She calls herself Maebh,' I said, 'and her man goes by the name of Master Henbane.'

The quill pen fell from his fingers, spattering the parchment, and Conor stared at me.

'Maebh? And would she be the owner of the blackest hair and the bluest eyes and the whitest skin in the whole universe? And does she occasionally take the form of a large black and white bird?'

'A magpie, yes.'

'And would this Henbane be a slimy, untrustworthy character with nasty little wee teeth on him?'

'He would.'

'Then to be certain, Tan'ith of Ynys Haf, if we can agree terms, then I shall help you.'

10

The change of attitude was so sudden that Nest's jaw dropped. She recovered herself immediately, and closed her mouth.

'Thank you, Lord Conor,' I said politely. Then all at once I got fed up with all the posh, formal talk. 'It sounds as if you know this Maebh person,' I said.

'Oh, to be sure I do. I have known her for many hundreds of years. Once we were friends, but – I will say only that she fell in with bad companions and was, ah, influenced.'

'She was? How? If you wouldn't mind sharing that with us, Lord Conor,' I said politely, as a sharp kick on the shins from Nest reminded me to guard my language. She was right, of course. I do have that terrible habit of letting my tongue run off like a rabbit. Dad says it's 'tongue off and running, brain left behind'. If I carried on with the weird talk, it might help me to remember who I was speaking to, so there was sense in it, I suppose.

'Let me tell you first about your man Henbane,' Conor said, leaning back in his high-backed chair. 'That wee fellow is Maebh's Uncle, and related to some person from your side of the Middlesome Sea. A fox-haired, stocky fellow, with not much in the way of wits but plenty in the style of ambition, he has.'

'Rhiryd Goch!' Nest and I said together.

'Aye. That would be the name. I understand from my messengers –' (*Spies*, I thought) 'that your man himself has given up the ghost and is dead altogether. But his sons are not, and they number three.'

'Rhiryd ap Rhiryd Goch, Ardwyn and Jason,' I said. 'I have heard of them, and seen ap Rhiryd.'

'Did you know they were all three raised in Henbane's household?' Conor enquired. 'Without doubt they are after the things that their father was wanting. Henbane wants Ynys Haf, and has used Maebh –' he almost spat the name out – 'to try to get it.'

Out of the corner of my eye, I suddenly noticed that the great flat mirror was changing, swirling with colour, turning deep crimson, rich blue, and greens ranging from emerald to forest. 'Lord Conor,' I went on, one eye on the mirror, 'who is Maebh? If-you-will-be-so-kind-as-to-tell-us,' I gabbled, after a Look from Nest.

'If you are one of the Daughters of the Moon, Lady, then she is your third cousin seventeen times removed.' (*But who's counting?* I thought. Obviously family trees were important to leprechauns.) 'Her mother was – let me see, now – your Great-Great-Great-Aunt DisGrace. A difficult lady, that one, with a finger in every magical pie, and I was forced to – well, never mind.' He showed small, even teeth in a smile that had no amusement in it. 'After I did what I had to do, Henbane took the child. He raised her, but not well. She grew up, and became so beautiful that she could still the wind in the trees.' There was a strange look on his face, regretful, remembering.

The mirror flickered, and suddenly, looking back at me, there was a face that I recognised. Astarte Perkins.

'Ah!' Conor said, leaning forward. 'You will be interested in this.'

We all three turned our eyes to the great mirror and paid attention. Astarte – who was now one of the million croaking frogs in Ynys Haf – was sitting at a table. In front of her was a great thick book that glowed with red, pulsating, evil light, as if it were thickly coated with creepy-crawlies. I had seen that book before. The Grimoire. The book crammed full of evil spells that the Circle of Seven Daughters of the Moon had successfully taken from her and sealed in Aunt Ant's dungeon. I began to worry, until I realised that, in the mirror, Astarte was only about twelve years old. Still gingery, rat-faced and odd-eyed, but only young.

A sinister figure appeared in the mirror behind her: tall, her hair piled on her head in a great black coil like a boa-constrictor. *Merch Corryn Du* – Spiderwitch. Astarte turned to look at her Great-Great-Great-Grandmother, her face sulky, and said something to her that was obviously not what the Spiderwitch wanted to hear, because her hand shot out, blood-red nails glistening, and clouted Astarte very hard around the ear. Sullenly, Astarte bent back to the book, one hand holding her face where her loving Granny's hand had swiped her, and the picture changed again.

This time, Astarte was a little older, and another girl was sharing her lessons. This child had hair black as night's wing, blue eyes and white skin, and was unmistakably Maebh, only Maebh aged about eleven. Spiderwitch was once again acting as their teacher, and just as Astarte had sulked, so did Maebh. She'd probably been spoiled rotten, being so pretty. But Maebh threw not only a tantrum, but the Grimoire as well. She picked it up and hurled it across the room. If it had hit the wall on the far side it would surely have exploded, with evil spells flying everywhere, and goodness knows what might have happened then. But *Merch Corryn Du* was quicker, and she threw magic at the wall to cushion the impact. So the hideous red book floated gently and unharmed back down to the table.

And then the witch turned her attention to Maebh. I recognised the look in the crimson-masked eyes, and shuddered. The tall, black-robed witch pointed her finger at the trembling girl and spoke. Maebh disappeared, and in her place sat a large, handsome bird. Astarte's magpie.

'Do you understand the way of it now, at all?' Conor asked, leaning back against the carved wood, one forefinger stroking his upper lip.

'I think I do,' I said. 'After my Aunts captured the Grimoire, Spiderwitch sent Astarte to get it back. When Astarte failed, and we got rid of her once and for all, Maebh was able to shift back from being a magpie – I'm not exactly sure how, but perhaps it was because there was no power left to keep her in bird-shape. Then, she and Henbane decided to come to Ynys Haf themselves. So they are no doubt trying to get the Grimoire back, as well as control Ynys Haf. Of course, they don't know –' I was going to say 'Aunt Ant's got the Grimoire', but I stopped myself just in time – 'um, where it is,' I finished. No point in telling Conor anything I didn't have to.

'I imagine you are right,' Conor said. 'But there is one thing you do not know.'

'And will you tell me, Lord Conor of the Land Beneath, what is that?' I asked. I had a feeling that we had come to the crunch. This would be where I must watch my words very carefully indeed.

He smiled, his eyes watchful, his small teeth gleaming. 'Aah,' he breathed. 'And what will you give me if I tell you? To be sure, knowledge is a most wonderful thing to possess, especially when I have it and you do not.'

Now, if Nest hadn't warned me, I might have thought the small man was joking, but I knew he wasn't. His fingers were steepled again, now, concealing his mouth, and his golden, owl-like eyes stared watchfully at me. Waiting.

Once, I might have blurted, 'whatever you want – anything, just tell us,' but I was older and wiser. I took a deep breath and tried to will my mind into the *feeling* of Ynys Haf, trying to get the Island of Summer's sensations into my head. I had to choose my words very, very carefully. Suddenly, the right words came, and I calmed down a bit. I could do this. I could be every bit as sneaky and devious as Conor could. I was the Lady, right?

'Lord Conor of the Land Beneath,' I began, 'tell me what you want from me, and I shall judge if I have the power to give it.'

Nest, who had tensed like a coiled spring, relaxed slightly. T.A. was staring from me to Conor and back again, an expression very like terror on her face.

'I could ask for half your land, but you have none

until Gwydion Dragonking is freed. I could ask for the Grimoire, but who knows where it has gone? I could ask for the Emerald Spellorium, which has been handed down from daughter to daughter for centuries in your family. Or for your first-born child. But you are half-human, and have doubtless been reared on tales of evil leprechauns and changeling children, and would not agree to that at all. So, Tan'ith of Ynys Haf. What shall I ask?'

'Tell me what you would like, Lord Conor. I repeat, if it is in my power, and will not harm Ynys Haf or the people, you shall have it.' Nest kicked me, and I knew I'd said something wrong. But what?

Conor clapped his hands, suddenly, and laughed, as if an idea had just come to him. Why was it I had the feeling he was two steps ahead of me the whole time?

'I know. It is a small thing, and in your power to give me if you succeed in finding your Dragonking. I want Maebh. But I want her with her cat-claws drawn.'

I raised my eyebrows. 'I don't quite understand.'

'When all this is finished, when the Dragonking is back on his throne, you will give me Maebh. I am a leprechaun: my magic is based in earth and sky, fire and water . . .' (*and mischief,* Ynys Haf said inside my head, quietly.) '. . . But your magic is different. 'Earth, sky, fire and water, true, but also the other world. The one above and beyond. I want Maebh, but I want her without a trace of her magic. I know you can do this.'

'You want her mortal?' I wasn't sure what he was getting at.

Conor shook his head. 'Oh no, my Lady. Not

95

mortal. Immortal, but without her magic. That will be my payment for telling you what I know. Take it or leave it. Take my bargain and know, leave my bargain and go.' He chuckled, showing those small, sharp teeth again. He was mesmerising.

I glanced at Nest, raised an eyebrow questioningly. Imperceptibly, she nodded.

'I agree. When I have Maebh in my power, you shall have her. So, Conor of the Land Beneath, what is it that you know?'

A smile had drifted across his golden face. It wasn't pleasant. I began to wonder if I had made a mistake, promising him Maebh. Why would he want her? Perhaps once he had been in love with Maebh – if such a person as Conor could love – and she had dumped him. And now he wanted her back. I should not like to be in Conor's power, with or without magic. For all his handsomeness, Conor of the Land Beneath was as evil in his way as my enemies were.

'I know that once, *Merch Corryn Du* the Spiderwitch and Henbane were married. Your Great Aunt DisGrace married their son, and their daughter married Rhiryd Goch. Maebh is Henbane's great-grand-daughter, and the sons of Rhiryd Goch are his nephews. Between them, Lady Tan'ith, they have powerful magic, and a fair claim to Ynys Haf through DisGrace.' He smiled, faintly. 'So, if you do not find Gwydion Dragonking, Henbane and Maebh will rule Ynys Haf. They will have the right of it and there will be nothing you can do.'

If I had been standing, my knees might have given way. I suddenly felt exactly what I was: a not very old girl completely out of my depth, sitting in an underground palace with a small but deadly ruler of a large, unruly and magical kingdom.

I took a deep breath and shut my eyes. I tried to tune in to Ynys Haf, to hear its music, but all that I heard was my heartbeat. I was on my own. Right, I said to myself. Now you know, and all you've risked is Maebh. Now what? I opened my eyes and looked at Nest. She was staring at me, her lips tight, willing me to do something. But what?

'If you want Maebh, Lord Conor, I must first free Gwydion.' I began. 'Do you know where he is?'

Conor smiled again. 'I do not. Would I not have told you at once, had I known?'

'Of course you would, Lord Conor,' (*in a pig's eye you would*, I thought) 'forgive me. But I don't know where in Ynys Haf to begin to look.'

'Perhaps he is not there,' Conor said, slyly. I stared at him. I hadn't even considered that he might be anywhere else.

'Indeed,' I said, feeling rather sick. If he wasn't in Ynys Haf he could be anywhere in the world. 'So, Lord Conor. Where shall I begin?'

In reply, Conor clapped his hands, and O'Liam of the Green Boots was beside him, glancing nervously from Conor to me. If anything went wrong, I hoped O'Liam wouldn't suffer for bringing Nest, T.A. and me into the Land Beneath.

'Yes, my Lord?' O'Liam said.

'O'Liam. Your cousin and her Lady need information. Take them to the Hermit of Glendalough. If your man the Hermit does not know, then there is no one in Erin who can help at all, to be sure.'

'The Hermit of Glendalough?' O'Liam said, disbelievingly, 'but –'

'The Hermit of Glendalough,' Conor repeated softly, almost whispering, his eyes half-closed, and O'Liam shut his mouth.

Whoever this hermit was, O'Liam wasn't exactly happy. I took a deep breath. Right. At least we could make a start. 'Thank you, Lord Conor of the Land Beneath. I shall' – good grief, where did *these* words pop up from? – 'be remembering you with grace at early birdsong, and think of you at bat-flight, and all the long bright hours in between. I am grateful to you.' I stood up. 'Come on, Nest, T– Haf.'

'Oh no, my Lady Tan'ith,' Conor said silkily. 'Lady Haf remains with me until you return.'

'What?' T.A.'s face was completely panic-stricken. I knew she was as anxious to get out of the Land Beneath as I was. 'But –'

Conor smiled, meeting my eyes, daring me. I opened and shut my mouth, feeling totally useless.

'It's all right, Tanz,' T.A. said in a little voice. 'Of course I'll stay. Look, no problem, OK? I'll be fine.' She turned to Conor and pinned a smile on her face. 'I'm sure I'll enjoy getting to know Lord Conor. Go on! Hurry up.' She made little shooing gestures, but her smile was frozen.

I exchanged glances with Nest. She looked as horrified as I felt. But there was nothing else for it. We had to leave T.A. behind.

11

As I left, I looked back. T.A. was sitting bolt upright, both hands clutching the arms of her chair, her short, dark hair gleaming in the candlelight. She gave me a little wave and a very wobbly smile.

'Come on, Nest,' I said through gritted teeth, 'the quicker we go, the quicker we'll be back.' I threw a last, false smile at Conor, who dipped his head politely, and showed his teeth. It wasn't a smile, though.

Outside, O'Liam was looking decidedly unhappy. 'Oh, oh, oh, why did I ever bring you here?' he lamented. 'To be sure it's an ill-wind blowing, and it never blowing me any good at all, not even if it blows me all the way to Galway and back!'

'Galway?' I said, 'is that where we're going?'

'No, of course it's not, woman,' O'Liam said crossly. 'Who in his right mind would want to go to Galway? It's a strange style of place altogether, Galway. Did you not hear Himself say it was Glendalough we had to go?'

'Well I don't know where Glendalough is, do I?' I scowled at the little man. 'For goodn –'

I think Nest saw that I was losing my cool and jumped in. 'O'Liam, dear, of all the people Conor could have asked to guide us, I'm so glad it's you. I know we'll be in safe, brave hands with you.'

'Mmphm, well. If your witch-woman don't even know where Glendalough is, it's just as well you've got me, that's true as a trumpet. Now. Let this be

99

understood. You do what I say while you are with me, and don't even think of dancing off back to Innish whatever it is you come from without visiting Himself again, first. I'd never hear the last of it, I would not. They have a word for it, so – "there's a lot of weather in a March day".'

Pardon? I was beginning to realise that O'Liam was one of those people who are deep mines of weird sayings. He'd certainly lost me with that one.

Anyway, if he thought I was going to go and leave T.A. behind, he didn't know me.

'Absolutely, O'Liam,' I assured him. 'You're in charge, right?'

He looked at me suspiciously. 'Right. Are you ready, so?'

'Yes,' Nest said, 'But surely you aren't going to wear those gorgeous green boots for travelling, O'Liam? It would be such a shame to ruin them.'

O'Liam surveyed his wonderfully shod toes. 'Ah, you're right, you're right. I shall go now and change them and be back in a whisk of an owl's whatever.'

As soon as he had flickered along the corridor out of earshot, I opened my mouth to speak, but Nest shot her hand across it so fast that all that came out was a sort of strangled 'Mmmph.' She shook her head, and her lips formed the word 'later'. I nodded. I should have realised that Conor might be listening – or watching, perhaps, in that vast round mirror.

When O'Liam returned, wearing sturdy brown boots, he led the way above ground and into the open air. It smelled wonderful, of sunshine and leaf-mould, and I breathed in deeply.

'If we're away to Glendalough,' O'Liam began, 'then we must travel fast. We won't get there by nightfall, not at all, but we can find a place to sleep and be there by sun-top tomorrow.'

'Sun-top?' I got a vision of something strappy to wear in hot weather.

'Do you not speak your own language?' the little man said sarcastically. 'Sun-top, sun-top. Half-way between sunrise and sundown.'

'Oh,' I said, understanding. 'Noon.'

'Aye, you would call it something nonsensical, so,' O'Liam said. 'Now look, how are we going to get there? If you could fly at all, it would be much quicker.'

'We can fly,' I said, and shimmered into a fat rook. Nest, beside me, shifted too, and we cocked our heads and looked at our escort.

'Ah, look at the fine strong beaks on the pair of you!' he said nervously. 'Just don't be thinking of taking a wee peck at me, right? Don't forget, a friend in need is a friend in greed!'

I opened my beak to try to sort out his saying, but decided life was too short. O'Liam, seeing the length and sharpness of my beak, and how it stood out from the bare patch at the base of it, gazed at it, horrified, until Nest squawked at us to get a move on.

So, with O'Liam travelling at his fast, flickering run, and Nest and me swooping overhead keeping pace with him, we set off for Glendalough. My wings were getting stronger, but I was still glad when O'Liam whizzed to the top of a hill and sat down on a boulder. We fluttered down to perch beside him.

'As no doubt you'll have noticed,' O'Liam began, 'the sun is slithering down in its usual unreliable and furtive manner and presenting us with a whole lot of blackness. It isn't in me to travel where I can't see a hand's breadth at all, so I think it might be entirely a good –'

'– idea to stop for the night?' I squawked, beginning to feel that it would take until breakfast time for him to get to the point.

'Exactly,' O'Liam agreed, giving me a dirty look. 'There's a sheltered spot just beyond, and we'll build a fire and eat.' He flickered away and we shifted and followed him on foot. It couldn't exactly be called a cave, more a deep hollow in the mountainside, but it would shelter all three of us easily, and we could build our fire in the entrance.

'I suppose you didn't bring any food with you?' he asked hopefully, when we had collected wood and made a fire.

We hadn't, but hey, I'm a witch, right? I can magic up a bit of food. It was in the rules, after all – I could use my magic for myself if it was a real emergency. And I was starving, and our guide was starving – and if that isn't an emergency, what is?

'Tell me, O'Liam, if you could have anything at all to eat, what would it be?'

The leprechaun closed his eyes ecstatically. 'Oh, Lady, I spend my whole natural life in the Land Beneath, and I don't get a whole lot of fish, I do not. And to my mind the nicest fish of all is a wee, silver, slippy herring, all roly-polied in fine oatmeal, and fried in a bit of butter and ate altogether with fresh bread and some more of the same. And a mug of hot minty tea to wash it down.' He opened his eyes. 'And as my Mammy used to say, listen to the river and you'll get a trout, so.' He put his head on one side. 'Can you hear a river, now, or must I go without my fish again?'

I concentrated hard, and seconds later a shower of fat herring fell out of the sky. One bounced off O'Liam's head and he caught another in both arms, clutching it comically like a large baby. I was pleased to see that the fish were not only dead but also cleaned, rolled in oatmeal and ready to cook.

'Oh, Lady, thank you!' O'Liam found a long stick and began threading fish onto it, his pointed little face beaming happily.

'Nest? What would you like?'

'Cheese, bread, apples – and some hot broth, Tansy, please. It's getting colder now that the sun's gone down.'

I magicked that, and then food for myself. I didn't have to think about it: Big Mac, large fries and coke, what else? As I bit into the burger (and *my* Big Macs are a hundred times better than the real thing, trust me!) O'Liam glanced up, his chin greasy with buttery fish, wiped his fingers on his jerkin and grinned ecstatically.

'Lady, these fish was born and swimming to make me happy, so they were,' he said, licking his lips. 'But they don't fill a person up entirely, you know. And while it's the quiet pigs that eat the meal, it's the loud ones that get second helpings. What might you be eating, all meaty and juicy there?' I sighed and

103

magicked another Big Mac, fries and coke. He took a tentative bite and sighed.

'Ooooh, Lady.' He didn't say another word until the entire lot had gone, then he gave a large, coke-y burp and fell asleep, the firelight glistening on his contented face.

'Well, there's a first,' I whispered, as Nest finished her apple and threw the core into a bush for the small creatures to finish. 'A leprechaun high on Big Macs and coke!'

'He'll be your friend for life if you carry on feeding him that way,' she whispered back. 'Which is just as well. At the moment he's Conor's creature, my cousin or not, but a leprechaun can usually be persuaded if you use the right words – or apparently the right diet!'

I grinned. Then I remembered. 'I just wish T.A. was with us. That rotten little –'

Nest frowned and put her finger to her lips. 'Remember the mirror, Tan'ith. While Conor has that he can see us wherever we are. He may be able to hear us, too. So be careful what you say.'

'That mirror's amazing, Nest. It puts our scrying bowl to shame, doesn't it? A bit like comparing a pocket telly with a flat-screen digital sixty-inch.'

Nest looked blank. 'I haven't got the faintest idea what you're talking about, Tansy.'

'It's – oh, never mind.' Life's too short to explain digital technology to a half-fairy!

'It used to belong to Merlin, that mirror,' she went on, 'but Merlin crossed Conor's path one day, quite by accident, and Merlin, for all his wisdom, has a tongue almost as unruly as your own. And of course he is male, and thinks he knows everything. But he didn't watch his tongue, and lived to regret it. Conor wanted the mirror, and he got it.'

I thought of Conor with new respect. If he could put one over on Gwydion's old tutor, he must be fairly foxy.

'Nest,' I said, carefully, 'can a Certain Crafty Person read and write?'

'Good gracious, no,' she said, and chuckled. 'Completely beneath his dignity. That's what he has all those wise men for. And they aren't too hot at it. Their spelling is atrocious.'

'Good,' I said, and picked up a stick. The floor inside the cave was soft and sandy, and I began to write in it.

'DO YOU THINK GWYDION IS IN IRELAND?' I scribbled, and rubbed it out when she had read it. She picked up a stick.

'I DON'T KNOW. IT'S POSSIBLE. BUT WHAT REALLY WORRIES ME IS FINDING THAT MAEBH HAS A CLAIM TO YNYS HAF.' She swooshed the sand flat again.

'SHE MIGHT HAVE A CLAIM, BUT I'VE GOT A BETTER ONE,' I wrote, 'AND WHILE I'M AROUND, SHE AIN'T GETTING IT!!!!'

'WE NEED TO FIND GWYDION. WITHOUT HIM YOU ONLY HAVE HALF A CLAIM.'

'HALF A CLAIM'S BETTER THAN NONE' I wrote. 'DO YOU THINK T.A. WILL BE OK WITH CONOR?'

Nest nodded. 'THE BIGGEST DANGER IS THAT HE MAY DECIDE TO MARRY HER BEFORE WE GET BACK.'

'What?' I was so shocked I didn't write that, I yelled it. O'Liam muttered and stirred in his sleep, and then settled again.

'DIDN'T YOU SEE THE WAY HE WAS LOOKING AT HER?' Nest wrote.

I shook my head. 'I WAS TOO BUSY TRYING NOT TO LAND US IN IT.'

'CONOR HAS AN EYE FOR A PRETTY FACE. AND T.A.'S IS.'

'BUT SHE'S MORTAL.'

'THAT WOULDN'T MATTER – WHILE SHE WAS YOUNG AND PRETTY, AT LEAST.'

I decided I liked Conor about as much as I could trust him. Not at all.

'DO YOU THINK HE'LL LET HER GO WHEN WE GO BACK FOR HER?'

Nest shrugged. 'WE MUST MAKE HIM, TANSY!'

All the same, I didn't get a whole lot of sleep that night. Mind, it wasn't all to do with worry. Indigestion from the Big Mac and O'Liam snoring helped.

There I was, dreaming that I was being chased by an elephant. I could feel the ground shuddering under its heavy thumping feet. Thudddd, thudddd, thuddddd! And then my eyes were open, a small hand was clamped tight over my mouth, and I was wide awake –

And the thudding kept right on jarring into my backbone.

12

O'Liam crouched beside me, his hand still covering my mouth. 'Be still as a stone, Lady,' he muttered. 'Don't be moving a whisker of your nostrils.' Carefully, his finger to his lips, he removed his other hand. Nest crouched silently on my left.

The ground vibrated against my backbone, and my wide eyes searched the blackness outside the cave. O'Liam tugged my sleeve, and slowly, slowly the three of us moved back into the deepest part of the cave, where the shadows were thickest and the moon couldn't reach.

The shattering thuds grew louder. Small pebbles dislodged from the rocky roof pattered down on our heads, and in the slightly paler outline of the cave mouth I could see the rock walls vibrate. The moon sailed out from behind a cloud, and the slope behind the cave became silvery. Nothing moved out there, yet still the gut-rocking, mind-numbing thuds went on. It sounded like one of those machines that road-menders use to bash the earth down flat before they tarmac it. Only about five thousand per cent louder.

And then the mouth of the cave went pitch dark. Something blotted out the moon. A warm, stinking wind roared into the cave, blowing my hair almost off my head. And then that same wind almost sucked us out of the cave mouth. I had to hang on to the walls with my finger- and toe-nails to stay put. I couldn't for the life of me think what was happening. A tornado?

An earthquake? And then, when a vast, questing finger snaked into the cave, its fingernail as large as a dustbin-lid, I knew . . .

I was about to meet my very first giant.

Nest scooted and slithered backwards, away from the finger, which was making scooping movements, the way you scrape chocolate cake mix out of a bowl, and when it slid towards me I had nowhere to go except up. I shifted into a bat and flew frantically outside. My radar kept me from flying into the giant, and I flittered past it and hovered, squeaking frantically, not believing the size of it. Forget King Kong on top of the Empire State Building. This *was* the Empire State Building, moving and breathing. While I watched, O'Liam suddenly lost his nerve and shot out of the mouth of the cave. The giant made a grab at him, and missed, and O'Liam shot between its fingers and disappeared into what looked like a badger's sett. He should be safe down there. But Nest was still in danger.

In a trice I changed into a golden eagle, and then realised my mistake: I was too big. The giant could catch me easily, the way a human might grab at a butterfly. So I changed rapidly into a long-eared owl, the only owl to live in Ireland (and oh, I hoped I'd carry on *that* tradition for at least the next few minutes!), and attacked.

I flew at the giant's eyes, pecking and flapping, and it fell over backwards, roaring with fury. Out of my round owl eyes I saw Nest scuttle out of the cave and change into a rabbit, scuttling down the nearest hole. Now that she and O'Liam were both safe I could save myself. I left off the attack and soared high into the night sky, my strong wings rowing the cool air, looking down on the giant.

Seeing it from a distance, I was able to take in the terrible size of it. And from up there, I realised that I had met it before. It was the Guardian of the Port. Somehow, she had scented our magic and followed us. But my, how she'd grown since I last saw her! She'd been a bit big and beefy then, but now!

After poking around for ages in trees and bushes, looking for us, the she-giant gave up and set off down the mountain, grumbling to herself. As soon as she had gone, I shifted into a rabbit and whizzed down the hole to tell Nest it was safe to come up, leaving an entire family of bunnies in a state of utter panic.

We headed for the sett, next, and were almost flattened by O'Liam shooting out of the hole at great speed, pursued by an extremely cross lady badger. O'Liam shot straight up a tree and clung there, wheezing, until she had shuffled, disgruntled, back into her home.

O'Liam's face was glowing white and his knees trembled and knocked when he finally came down from his perch.

'Oh, Lady, didn't I think my final last hour had come when herself showed up. It was almost like she knew I was there, with the nasty, knowing wriggle of her fingers and all. And then the great stripey bear creature was after killing me, and me not laying a hand on her cub at all, whatever she thought.'

'Did you recognise the giant?' I asked Nest.

She shook her head. 'I was too busy scooting down

a rabbit hole. Landed flat on top of a Papa Rabbit with a temper like nobody's business,' Nest said, ruefully. 'He went for me with feet and teeth. At one stage I was beginning to think I would be safer with the giant.'

'Giantess,' I said. 'Bearing a strange likeness to the large lady we met when we landed.'

Nest's eyes widened. 'That was the Guardian of the Port? She's a Changer? Now those *are* rare. In fact, I thought they'd all died out long ago. There are about half-a-dozen ordinary giants left, but if there's a Changer about, we'll really have to keep our eyes peeled. And I'm afraid there can't be any doubt at all, now. She scented our magic when we were in her cottage. It's her job to find us, and she will keep trying. A Changer. Well.'

'When you say "Changer",' I said, carefully, trying *very hard* not to get panicky, 'do you mean she can change the way we do? Into birds and animals and stuff?'

Nest laughed. 'No. Don't worry. All that Changers can change is their size.'

'Phew! That's a relief.' I'd been imagining 200-metre high red ants and stuff . . .

'What? What? What's a relief?' O'Liam squeaked. 'What are you talking on about? What?'

'Calm down, O'Liam dear,' I said, patting the little man's shoulders. 'It's only that when we got off the boat, we made a little, tiny mistake. We asked a lady for help, and it turns out that she's not only the Guardian of the Port and can sniff out magic, but she's also a giant who can change her size. She's sort of after us, so we'll have to take care. But don't worry. You guide us to the Hermit, and we'll take care of you.'

O'Liam turned paler than ever. 'You mean that was Big Deirdre the Port-watcher? She's after us? Herself? The Dreadful Deirdre? Oh, mercy be. Oh, why did I ever leave the Land Beneath?' he moaned, and sank down in a heap on the ground.

'Oh, come on, O'Liam, it's not as bad as all that, surely,' I said, trying to cheer him up.

'Oh, it is, it is, it is,' he wailed. 'Didn't Big Deirdre have a cub once, and didn't Conor hunt the poor creature until it died? She's certain death to any leprechaun that crosses her path. And now you're telling me it's us she's after? Oh, why don't I just lie down and die here, for if nothing else it will save time. Better the devil I don't know and I certainly know Big Deirdre.'

'Conor killed her baby?' I said. 'But that's terrible. Awful. How could he kill a baby anything, even if it was a giant?'

'A baby giant is the size of a tree,' O'Liam said, looking around him nervously, in case Conor might be listening, 'and Conor the Magnificent bravely hunted and killed it and isn't its stuffed head up there on the wall of his trophy room for all to admire?'

'Ugh!' I was beginning to like Conor less and less. 'That's sick!'

When O'Liam had pulled himself together with the aid of some grilled kippers and bread and butter and a boiled egg and toast soldiers and some strawberry jam and crumpets, the sun was up and we set off towards Glendalough.

111

We were there before noon, which was just as well, because O'Liam was beginning to get on my nerves. He wasn't flicker-running the way he had been the day before: he was twitching nervously about, peering all round him, walking backwards into trees, tripping over roots, until I got exasperated.

'Oh, for goodness sake, O'Liam,' I squawked out of my rook-beak, 'if Big Deirdre is around you'll hear her before you see her, won't you? There's no way she can creep up on you, that's for sure.'

O'Liam scowled at me. 'And isn't that all you know, you foreigner, you. Do you have giants in Innish-wherever-it-is you come from? No. You do not indeed, so. Then how do you know she isn't lying in wait pretending to be a mountain?'

'I think we'd spot her from up here, wouldn't we?' Nest said soothingly. 'Please, O'Liam, calm down. If we see the giant, I promise we'll shift you into something too small for her to see.'

'She'd smell me,' the little man said miserably. 'Sure as pigses earses, she'd smell me.'

And then we flew over a clump of trees and saw Glendalough. Now, I've seen Snowdonia from the bridge coming off Anglesey, and the glory of that stopped me in my tracks, but Glendalough was as spectacular in a different way.

A clear, peaceful lake stretched away as far as the eye could see, trees reflected in its stillness, scarcely a ripple breaking the surface. Dragonflies swooped and darted over their own mirror images, and yellow wagtails, swifts and swallows darted like living arrows above the water, feasting on tiny flies.

I was so taken with this vision that I almost flew into the Hermit's tower without noticing it. Only Nest's squawk of warning stopped me, and I swerved just in time to avoid crashing into the stone walls.

It wasn't quite what I'd been expecting. It was a fairly weird contraption: a tall, thin tower with arrow-slits in the walls and a door half way up it. A tall ladder hung from hooks beside the door, at a height where it could be reached from the door but not from the ground, which I supposed was one way to avoid unwanted guests!

O'Liam went to the foot of the tower while Nest and I shimmered into our own shapes, and I flexed my aching arms. Despite the sunshine there had been a bit of a head-wind, and I was tired from flying into it the whole way.

The leprechaun grabbed hold of a rope that disappeared into a small hole in the wall and yanked it, hard. A loud bell pealed inside the tower, and a family of rooks shot out of the roof, scattering loudly in all directions. I think they were swearing at us.

I waited for the Hermit to put in an appearance. And waited. And waited. Exasperated, O'Liam tugged the bell-rope again, and at last the door flew open. A head adorned with a knitted woolly hat poked out.

'Who is it? What do you want? Why are you here? Go away!'

'It is I, O'Liam of the Green Boots,' O'Liam said proudly. 'Emissary of Lord Conor of the Land Beneath. With Guests.'

'No, no it is not, no, not at all,' the head replied, and withdrew, slamming the door shut behind him.

O'Liam looked like a balloon that has had a pin stuck in it. Furiously he grabbed the rope and shook and shook it. The clangour echoed off the water and the hills all round. The door flew open again.

'Is it yourself again, pestering honest folks?'

'It is. It is I, it is O'Liam of the Breen Goots,' he gabbled. 'I mean, the Green Boots.' His golden face turned pinkish with embarrassment.

The face stuck out of the tower again. It was old and wrinkled and dirty, and appeared to have only one tooth in its head. What Dad might have called 'central eating'. Bit groanworthy, but there you go, that's Dad for you.

'How can you say you're O'Liam of the Green Boots when they're brown entirely?' asked the querulous fellow. 'Impostor, that's what you are. Liar. Go away.' And the door slammed shut again. O'Liam was almost in tears.

I decided it was time I exerted myself. I tried something I'd never done before. I half-shifted. That is I stayed me, but I grafted on a pair of large wings. What sort, I'm not sure. Possibly a South American condor, maybe the extinct Roc. They had to be big to take my weight, OK? Anyway, they did the trick, lifted me up to a level with the wooden door. It was old and cracked and dusty at close quarters, and there were spiders in the keyhole, although what good a keyhole is ten metres off the ground I can't imagine. I raised my fist and bashed on the door, sending dust and surprised spiders flying into space.

Slowly, cautiously, the door opened a crack and I floated back a bit to allow it to open fully. Then, eyeball to eyeball with the owner of the woolly hat, I scowled as fiercely as I could manage.

'Below,' I said, 'is The O'Liam of the Green Boots, whether he is wearing them or not. And The O'Liam is here on the orders of Lord Conor of the Land Beneath. And I am the Lady of Ynys Haf, and unless you invite us politely in, little woolly hat person, and make us welcome, and answer our questions as nicely as your mother must once have taught you, you will be a very sorry little woolly hat person.' I took a leaf out of Conor's book, half closed my eyes and hissed, 'Right?'

The face under the woolly hat stared. It blinked its eyes, and swallowed nervously. 'Right. Ah. Um. Do you say so?'

And then a querulous voice behind it said 'Padraig. For the love of all the bedraggled saints, will you shut the damn door? The draught's like a red-hot knife to my rheumaticals, so it is.'

'Ah,' said Padraig. 'You've a visitor, Hermit, so.' And stood back to allow me to fly in. I stood with my arms folded while Padraig lowered the ladder for Nest and O'Liam to climb up and join me, and then turned.

'Take me to your leader,' I said. D'you know, I've ALWAYS wanted to say that!

13

Padraig looked me up and down. 'What style of creature might you be when you're at home, with your big old wings, then?'

I folded them neatly behind me. 'I'm a witch, little man. Now. Where's the Hermit?'

'Ah. Sure I should be used to it by now, but this place is getting worse and worse. Witches now, is it? There goes the neighbourhood. Follow me, then, your witch-ship. That terrible grating, grinding sound you can hear is only my old bones in agony, so don't let it be worrying you, oh no.' He scuttled away up a spiral staircase in the corner of the room and we followed him up to the top of the turret.

The room was almost completely dark, and I couldn't see a thing. 'If there are any windows in here,' I suggested, 'you might like to open a couple.'

Padraig's shocked voice came out of the darkness. 'What? Open windows? Windows, open? With me feeling the cold the way I do and Himself old enough to be blowed away entirely?'

The creaky old voice I had heard earlier, spoke so close to me that I jumped. 'Open the shutters, Padraig. Let me see my visitors. Sure and they're the first I've seen in a terrible long while.'

'Open the shutters, Hermit?' Padraig said, 'but the shutters are never opened –'

'Padraig. Open the benighted shutters,' the voice said again.

'Yes, Master. But if we all collapse and die straight away with the galloping megrims, I'll have you know I will not myself be to blame.'

I heard him scuttle across the tower and suddenly a blinding flash of light shot across the room as he flung back the wooden shutter. When they were all open, I saw the owner of the creaky voice. He looked so old that even his wrinkles had wrinkles! He looked like a crumpled brown-paper parcel.

He was tiny, with a few white hairs sticking out from below a strange square cap. His blue eyes were almost concealed by bushy white eyebrows, and he was smiling. At least, I think he was smiling. The beard all but concealed not only his mouth but most of his body down to his knees. He was seated in a tall-backed wooden throne and he was staring at me.

'Ahem, ahem, um, oh,' he said creakily, as if he were unused to speaking. 'Does your Mammy go by the name of Gwenhwyfar, by any chance?'

I stared back at him. 'Yes. How did you know?'

'Ah, if you aren't the spit out of her mouth. And what might your name be?'

'Tan'ith,' I said, completely mystified. How on earth could he know my mother?

'Ah. Daughter of the Moon,' he said, and chuckled. 'You'll be a bit of a witch, then.'

'Yes.' I stared at him. The top of his hat seemed to be moving. And then, to my horror, I realised that it wasn't the top of his hat, it was a gigantic spider, and it had spun a web from his hat to the oak-beamed ceiling of the chamber. It was a large web, and bits of it were dusty, as if it hadn't been disturbed for ages

117

and ages. I looked around the chamber. It was possibly the dirtiest room I'd ever seen in my whole life, and that included Spiderwitch's underground cavern. Dust mice – no, dust *elephants* lurked in the curves of the round walls and cart-wheeled across the floor in the draught from the opened shutters. Spiderwebs draped the ceiling like thick veils, and whenever one of us moved thick dust stirred in clouds.

'I suppose you will be wanting to make the witch welcome,' Padraig grumbled. 'Will I put the kettle on?'

'You will so, Padraig,' the Hermit replied. 'And will you see if there is any left of that Christmas cake we were given fifty or sixty years back?'

'Ah, it's gone entirely, Master,' Padraig said regretfully. 'Didn't you have the very final piece yourself and leave none, no, not a scrap or a crumb, for me. And wasn't it the tastiest bit of –'

'I don't want a drink, thank you very much,' I said firmly, 'until this place has been cleaned up. Right, Nest?'

'Right.'

And so we rolled up our sleeves and got on with the job. We could have magicked it, I suppose, but magic, according to Mam and the Aunts, never does the corners properly. We set O'Liam to lighting a fire and boiling water, and Padraig scrambling to find brooms and rags that we could use to clean up the old man's tower. I suppose it's Mam's influence that makes me hate dirt. Untidiness I can stand, (you should see my bedroom!) dirt I can't. We swept and dusted and hooked down cobwebs, and I personally (brave or

118

what?) removed the arachnid from the top of the Hermit's hat and chucked it out of the arrow-slit. When the room was cobweb-free and shining, I produced a tea-table laid with a lace cloth, hot tea, scones, applecake, Welsh cakes and thickly buttered *bara brith,* all out of thin air. Padraig was most impressed.

'Would there be any soda bread at all?' O'Liam said hopefully, so of course there was.

I would have liked to suggest the Hermit took a bath before his tea, but he might have died of shock, so I had to content myself with brushing off the worst of the spidery traces with a pink feather duster.

Padraig managed very well considering he only had one tooth. I had to refill the plates several times, and O'Liam wasn't far behind Padraig. There was one piece of *bara brith* left, and they each eyed it and each other while they chewed. Padraig won, which made around two dozen slices by my reckoning.

'This curranty, buttery bread stuff is pleasant,' he said, 'and the applety stuff also, but I imagine it will bring on my indigestion something powerful.'

'Probably,' I said. 'But it will be the twenty-fourth slice that caused it, I expect.'

When everyone was full, I cleared away the dishes and disappeared them. No point in washing up if I don't have to. Magic's perfectly OK for that, thanks very much. I was looking forward to a long chat with the Hermit, but in the way of old people, as soon as he had eaten, he fell asleep. Padraig was already asleep with his one-toothed mouth wide open, his hands clasped on his little pot-belly and his woolly hat cock-eyed on his head.

I whispered to Nest, 'Do you think the Hermit will wake up soon?'

She shook her head. 'Doubt it. I think the best thing we can do is leave the pair of them, make up some beds for ourselves in the downstairs room and get some sleep.'

We spiralled downstairs to the newly-cleaned room and I produced three sleeping bags and three air mattresses (already blown up: do you think I'm daft?) and we got down to some serious sleeping ourselves. O'Liam chose the emerald green sleeping bag, and was very taken with the zipper. He spent about twenty minutes whizzing it up and down until Nest got irritated and made him stop. The sulky silence that followed turned rapidly into a gentle snore, and at last we slept.

We were woken by Padraig in the doorway, clearing his throat. 'Ahem? Would you be ready for some breakfast now, your Witchship? The Hermit is awake and hungry. So if you're ready to eat he'd be wholly grateful if you would be so kind as to join him straight away, now, immediately and at once.'

We scrambled out of our bags and washed our faces, then went up the stairs to see the old man. He was sitting hopefully, knife and fork in hand, at an empty table.

'Would there be bacon at all?' he asked. Well, what do you think? And eggs, and pork sausages and fried bread and grilled tomatoes and mushrooms and baked beans. He loved the beans. He'd never had them before. When he'd finished, I kept talking to him so he wouldn't drop off again. That was the last thing we wanted, having to go through the eat-and-sleep routine again. We'd be here until Christmas if we did. That reminded me. I magicked a cake tin full of iced Christmas cake and put it underneath his chair for later.

'Now,' he said, wiping egg yolk off his whiskers. 'What is it that you want, daughter of Gwenhwyfar? Ah, she was a girl, that one, she was so!' He chuckled happily, and rubbed his knobbly old hands together.

I made a mental note to cross-examine Mam about this when I got back!

I explained what had happened to Gwydion, and why we were there.

'This Maebh,' the old man said slowly, 'would she be a black-haired young woman with eyes like the sky and skin like snow?'

I sighed. 'She would.' It would be great to be described in such flattering terms myself. And Maebh was a baddie!

'Ah. And was there a wee, slippery type of a man with her? Name of Henbane?'

I nodded.

'Nasty piece of work, that one. You'll be needing to watch him close, now.'

'Mmm. The trouble is, Master Hermit, that unless we can find Gwydion, then Henbane could very well take over Ynys Haf. And that would be awful.'

'It would indeed. It is always a bad thing when the nasty ones in any world prosper. The question is, where is Gwydion Dragonking?'

I already knew the question. What I wanted was the answer, for goodness sake!

'Let me think.' And the old gentleman folded his arms across his full tummy and fell asleep.

'Oh, great!' I whispered to Nest. 'What do we do now?'

'Wait until he wakes, I suppose,' Nest said. 'Goodness knows how long that will be.'

'Excuse my forwardness for speaking, your witchship,' said Padraig, 'but when Master Hermit rests his eyes he's usually dreaming seriously. You'll need to wait until he opens them again.'

'Dreaming' I said, doubtfully. 'Oh.'

'Dreaming seriously, I said. There's a difference, you know. Tell me, would there be any of that curranty bread left at all, your Witchship?' Padraig asked hopefully. 'Only I've a powerful old pain in the right quadrant of my left leg and I'm sure a piece of that good stuff would cure it.'

About two hours and four loaves of buttered *bara brith* later, while the sun moved round from arrow-slit to arrow-slit in the tower, Nest and I were still sitting patiently waiting and twiddling our thumbs. O'Liam went to play with the zip of his sleeping bag again. And then the old man's eyes fluttered open.

'Tea,' he croaked, and Padraig put the kettle on. When he had slurped a mugful, and spilled some down his beard, he sat up straight in his chair and smiled at me. 'I know where your Dragonking is!' he said happily.

Relief! I felt a huge grin spread across my face. 'Wonderful!' I said. 'Where?'

'Oh,' the old man said. 'He's in a cavern.'

'We know that already,' I said, the grin slipping a bit. 'But where?'

'Ah. Did you want to know that also?' the old man said, frowning so that his white eyebrows meshed like knitting.

I nodded, slowly.

'Ah,' he said again, and folded his arms and closed his eyes again.

I stared helplessly at Nest, wondering how many hours we should be stuck here, with Gwydion lost and T.A. in the clutches of a sneaky leprechaun king. But only a few minutes later the faded eyes were open again.

'He's in a cavern,' he said, 'where the flowers meet the toad and the river meets the road, and the sky meets the sea and the wind blows free.'

'Oh,' I said blankly. I'd hoped that he'd say, 'turn left out of here, keep going for a mile and a half and right next to Farmer O'Reilly's dung-heap, you'll find the entrance to a cave,' or something like that. But he hadn't.

I sighed and frowned. 'But where,' I said, trying to keep the frustration out of my voice, 'do the flowers meet the toad? In Ireland? In Ynys Haf? In my time Wales? In Timbuktoo? Where?'

'Well, it isn't that wholly outlandish Timbuktoo place. And it isn't Erin. And it isn't your Time Wales. So it must be –'

'Ynys Haf!' I said triumphantly.

'Yes. And no,' the old man said, and closed his eyes again.

'There now!' Padraig said. 'You have your answer. Wasn't it a fine answer, too, with the rhyming bits and all, so?'

I stared exasperatedly from smug Padraig to the gently snoring ancient Hermit and wanted to tear my hair out. 'Is that all the answer I'm going to get?' I asked. 'Is that it?'

'I think,' Nest said softly, 'that's it. But I think it's all we need.'

'It is?'

She nodded. 'We'd better go, now. We must get T.A. and leave Erin as fast as we can.'

'But do you really think you know the place where Gwydion might be?'

She smiled. 'I think so. If you read between the lines, and you know Ynys Haf.'

'Then what are we waiting for? Let's get out of here, get T.A. and go home.'

We went to get O'Liam, who had crawled into his emerald sleeping bag and was fast asleep with his thumb in his mouth.

'Is it time to go, now?' he asked sleepily when I shook him. 'Do you have your answers? Will we go back to the Land Beneath?'

I nodded, and he grinned. Then he crawled out of his sleeping bag and gazed at it sadly. 'I do surely wish I had one of them things, so I do. Is it not a wonderful invention, being warm to sleep inside and wonderful entertainment also, I shall miss the convenience of it, I shall. A bag in the hand is worth two in the bush, it is.'

So we took it with us, rolled up and tied with string to O'Liam's back, as his reward for being our guide.

14

Following O'Liam's flickering shape was much easier than it had been on the outward journey, because now he was wearing a sleeping bag of a shade of green that had no possible place in nature even in Ireland, and was simple to spot!

By nightfall we were more than two-thirds of the way back, and well past the place where the giant Deirdre had almost caught us. Personally, I was trying rather hard not to think about Big Deirdre, and was hoping she'd forgotten all about us.

'Nest,' I squawked, as we flapped along above O'Liam's head, 'we aren't going back by boat, are we?'

'It would be better if we did. We won't be so tired when we get back if the boat has done all the work.'

'You might be. I get seasick, remember? And being seasick is exhausting, trust me. Besides, if we go back the same way as we came, then we will have to go past Deirdre again. And she won't miss us this time.'

'You're right. But we won't talk about this now, Tansy. Remember Conor.'

I did. How could I forget? But I took her point.

Just as the sun began to die, O'Liam stopped on the banks of a small, clear river, and dropped his sleeping bag on the ground. We perched next to him and shifted.

'Do you think,' he said, hopefully, peering into the clear brownish waters, 'that this little river might have a trout or two swimming in it? Trout that might be prepared to give up the ghost for my sake?'

'It might,' I said, and shifted into a large grey heron. Within seconds I was wading in the icy shallows, and moments later two large brown trout flapped on the bank.

'And would there be any of them remarkable meaty, squishy things you were eating?'

I sighed. 'And how about ice-cream for afters, O'Liam?'

'Scream? Now why would you want to do that?'

'No, not I scream, ice – oh, never mind. Just wait until you've finished your trout and see. Nest, what would you like?'

When Nest's venison was eaten, and my fish and chips, and O'Liam's second course, I produced a monster Knickerbocker Glory, topped with cream and a cherry. I had one myself, too, but Nest contented herself with some wild strawberries.

O'Liam eyed the pink and white concoction warily. 'Now, what would I be doing with a great big thing like that, Lady?'

'You pick up a spoon, like this, O'Liam, and you dig in. Try it.'

O'Liam had a bit of trouble relating to the long spoon – he muttered something about supping with the devil – but as the first icy mouthful trickled down his throat, his eyes closed in ecstasy. 'Ooooh!' he said, and then 'Aaaah!'. The dessert disappeared in record time, and the little man lay back, his eyes half-closed.

'That,' he said, dreamily, 'was as much like eating a cold cloud as anything at all. I just hope we shan't be running into the giant again, for I'm too full up to move an inch, and it's a long road with a stomach turning.'

I made a mental note to sit down and try to untangle his sayings for him – some time.

Well, Deirdre didn't come in the night, thank goodness, and after breakfast next morning (which was rainy and a bit on the chilly side) we set off to rescue T.A.

It isn't a lot of fun flying in the rain, even if one's feathers are nicely waterproofed. The trouble is that there's always just enough girl in me not to like wet weather. 'I hate rain!' I squawked at Nest. 'I'll be glad when we can get inside and out of it.'

'Rain?' O'Liam said, flickering behind an oak tree, 'this isn't rain. This is just a soft day. Rain is when it comes down like iron bars. It never rains unless it pours. Sure and this is just sea-mist, so.'

I was about to make a rude comment about the difference between mist and rain when something vast suddenly appeared in front of me. Startled, I back-pedalled in mid-air, and managed to avoid crashing into it. O'Liam yelled 'every man for himself!' and hurled himself (painfully, by the shrieks) into a patch of brambles, but Nest wasn't so lucky. Perhaps her reflexes were slower than mine, because Big Deirdre was able to snatch her out of the air when Nest crashed into her chest.

The giantess held Nest cupped in her hands, and applied one large eye to the (relatively) small hole between her thumbs.

'And what does Missus Deirdre have here?' she

rumbled. 'Is it a rook, at all, or would it be something else? If it's a rook, then Missus Deirdre shall squash it, she shall, or maybe she shall eat it. But if it's a witch, then who knows what she shall do to it? Missus Deirdre hates witches almost as much as she hates lepperycorns!'

I considered flying down and pecking her eyes out, but then she might hurt Nest.

The giantess transferred Nest into her left hand, which she held loosely clenched, and bent down to the brambles, poking around in it with her forefinger, which was the size of a small telegraph pole. 'Are you in there, little man? Will you not be polite and come out and give us the sociable greeting?'

O'Liam's voice was trembling. 'I will not, so. I am not here at all.'

'What if I stamp on the bush, little man?'

'Then I shall be dead entirely. But I am not coming out. Because I tell you I am not here.'

Deirdre flicked the bush very hard, and O'Liam shrieked. Suddenly, Deirdre's expression changed from glee to surprise, and she stared at her left hand. 'Ouch!' she bellowed, and her voice made leaves fall off trees for miles around. 'Ouch!' she repeated. 'What's that sticking into me?' She opened her hand, and Nest stood on the palm of it, her hair whipping round her face in the gale of the giant's breath, her face furious. In her right hand she held a sword.

Big Deirdre's face changed again. It went from pain to disappointment, all in one go. 'Oh,' she said. 'It isn't the witch at all.'

'No it isn't,' Nest said. 'It's me, the Princess Nest of

Ynys Haf, cousin to O'Liam of the Green Boots, Emissary of Conor of the Land Beneath, and I am Aunt to both the Lady and the Dragonking of Ynys Haf, and if you don't let us go immediately you will be sorry.'

'Will I so? And who will tell them if I squish and squash you flat as a cowpat?' Big Deirdre's hand was beginning to close again, and I frantically searched around for something useful to do. Suddenly I had an idea. I'd never tried it before, and I wasn't sure that I could manage it. However, I thought hard and concentrated harder – and although I almost bust a blood vessel doing it, and certainly gave both my knees a bit of a wrench, landing, I suddenly changed from a small rook to a very large giantess. About ten metres taller than Deirdre, to be exact, and standing behind her.

'**I WILL!**' I thundered, very close to her left ear, and I was rather pleased to see her drop Nest, who shifted back to a bird on her way down, and landed safely on O'Liam's bramble bush. Big Deirdre jumped about twenty metres into the air.

'Oh, by the hairs of my Mammy's beard, who are you?' Deirdre whimpered, clutching her ear.

'**I,**' I said, '**AM YOUR VERY WORST NIGHTMARE, BIG DEIRDRE!**' And of course, I was. She didn't often see people bigger than herself.

'Oh,' the giantess said in a very small voice (for a giantess, that is), 'if you'll let me go I promise I'll be good.'

I scowled ferociously. '**SEE THAT YOU ARE! OR ELSE!**'

Honest, I almost scared myself. **'NOW, DEIRDRE, *SCRAM!'***

She scrammed. As the thunder of her footsteps died into the distance, O'Liam, dusty and covered in small scratches, backed carefully out of his brambles.

'Could you not have done that before I leapt into the thornybits, so?' he complained, peering up at me. 'A leprechaun in the hand is worth two in the thornybush, so it is.'

'Look, O'Liam,' I reminded him as I shifted back to my own size, 'you didn't get eaten, did you?'

'That's entirely true,' he said. 'Entirely. I can't argue with that at all.'

Nest joined us, shimmering into her own shape. 'Now,' she said, 'let's go and rescue T.A.'

Personally, I couldn't wait.

We were back at the little door in the oak within an hour, and followed O'Liam down into the Land Beneath. The first thing he did was take his precious sleeping-bag and put it in his quarters, and return with his emerald, sparkling boots on his feet.

'Time to go and see Conor,' I said, mentally rolling up my sleeves.

O'Liam looked shocked. 'Absolutely not!' he said, shaking his head. 'Not at all. Not now, at quarter-past-rose-close. Sure, isn't it time for his dancing lesson?'

'His what?' I stared at the little man.

'His dancing. Remarkably keen on the dance, you know, Lord Conor is. A master at it, if I may say so. And he must not be interrupted until the hour has passed.'

'When will that be?'

'Why, when he's finished the lesson, of course. Could be today, could be tomorrow –'

I shook my head, needing to clear it. I seemed to have got lost somehow. 'But you said –'

'An hour,' Nest supplied. 'But leprechaun hours – especially Lord Conor's leprechaun hours – are a bit on the fluid side.'

'So we wait?'

Nest nodded. 'We wait.'

We seemed to be doing an awful lot of waiting, one way and another.

O'Liam fetched us food and drink, and the bright, tiny girls helped us wash the dust from our bodies and change our clothes, which all helped to pass the time. At last enough of it had passed for Conor to be ready to see us.

This time, while my breeches and tunic were being laundered (I hoped, anyway) I wore a deep chestnut brown velvet gown which, and I'm not being big headed about this, honest, (well, maybe just a bit) showed off my auburn (yes, auburn, NOT red) hair and made my freckles almost disappear. I swept as regally as I could manage into Conor's chamber, and bowed my head briefly.

Conor bobbed his own, slightly, in return. I looked around the room for T.A.

'The Lady Haf?' I enquired politely.

'Is resting,' Conor said smoothly. 'Did you find the Hermit well?'

'As well as can be expected, Lord Conor, for one so very old.'

'They say his mind is wandering with the great age of him. Is it so?'

'I found his mind keen enough, Lord Conor.' I was trying to ungrit my teeth.

'Then you learned what you needed to learn?'

Nest was standing slightly behind me, and to my right, and her left fore-finger suddenly poked, hard, into my ribs.

'Owoh!' I squeaked, and thought before I spoke. 'It is possible that we may have, Lord Conor. But sadly, as you say, he is old. Perhaps his mind only seemed keen. Perhaps his wits are wandering. Perhaps his advice was useless.' I sighed, looking tragic. I do that quite well, my Mam says.

King Conor of the Land Beneath steepled his fingertips again. 'Hmm. And where did he say you might find your Dragonking?'

Suddenly, in my nostrils came the sweet smell of Ynys Haf. The unpolluted air, the freshness of spring flowers, the green smell of grass and the musky smell of leaf-mould in autumn. Ynys Haf was telling me something. So I lied.

'In the Dragon Mountains to the North of Ynys Haf, Lord Conor. That is where Gwydion Dragonking sleeps, according to the Hermit. Now,' I smiled sweetly, meeting his eyes, 'if you will tell Lady Haf we're ready to go, we shall thank you most sincerely,' (*not*, I thought) 'and be on our way.'

'And if Lady Haf wishes to stay?'

15

'What? Stay?' Nest's finger collided with my ribs again. 'I mean, of course she would be honoured to stay for ever in your glorious presence, Lord Conor, but I think she would probably like to go home '

'We shall see.' Conor clapped his hands. The nasty, smirky little smile was back again. It was the sort of smile that made me want to smack it, very hard. It also made me worry. A tiny female leprechaun shot down the corridor and, shortly afterwards, returned with T.A.

'Hi, Tanz,' she said, brightly. She looked as if she hadn't a care in the whole wide world.

'Hi, T- er, Haf,' I said, slowly, staring at her, hard. There was something in her eyes that wasn't quite right. 'We're ready to go home, now.'

Her face fell. 'Oh. Must we? I don't want to go home.' She tripped past me and went and sat in the high-backed chair next to Lord Conor, leaning towards him, matily. 'I'm only just getting to know dear Conor properly. I think I shall stay a little longer. You and Nest go on back. I'll follow later, all right?'

I tried to imagine what would happen if I went back to Ynys Haf without her. Even worse, if I went back to My Time Wales without her. 'No, Haf, you have to come with us. Now.'

Conor's voice was silk over steel. 'But you heard Lady Haf. She wishes to stay.' And he lifted her hand and kissed her fingertips. T.A.'s eyes almost crossed with delight. Talk about moon-struck!

Then I heard Nest's voice in my head. *'He's bewitched her, Tansy. Quick, shift her, grab her and fly.'*

I didn't stop to argue. As Nest flickered into a sparrow-hawk I shifted T.A. into a mouse, shifted myself, and grabbed her gently in my beak. Then we were winging through the winding corridors, hurtling past astonished leprechauns, who flattened themselves against the earthen walls as we flashed by, Conor's angry voice shrieking orders in our wake. As I was flying, I was thinking furiously: what if the door is closed? *What if the door is closed?*

But as we reached it, O'Liam was there, flinging it wide so that we could escape. 'Go, Nest,' he screamed. 'Go Lady!' Behind him I could see leprechauns bearing down on him. I knew that Conor would punish him terribly for what he had done. So I shifted him. Seconds later there were three of us flying: Nest, O'Liam and me, and struggling furiously in my sharp beak, T.A., who was the only one not pleased to be out of there.

There was no possibility of taking a boat to Ynys Haf. Any boatman who carried us, Conor would find and make him suffer. So like it or not, we had to fly. We flew swiftly, and kept alert – all the time waiting for Conor, somehow, to try to stop us.

We approached the coast, and I tightened my grip on the wriggling rodent in my beak. It was squeaking furiously, but it was anger, not fear. I sent a thought-wave to it. 'Keep still, T.A., or I shall drop you in the sea.'

What she thought-waved back was unprintable, I'm afraid. I didn't know my friend knew words like that!

Whatever spell Conor had put on her, it was a strong one.

It was hard, flying for mile upon mile across open sea carrying her in my beak, because she wriggled every wing-flap of the way. My neck was aching, and the pull of the muscles across my back was murder. We skimmed the wave-tops, because higher up the wind was stronger, flying above deep grey water, which lightened to blue as, at last, after a journey that felt like about ten thousand miles, we reached Cantre'r Gwaelod's sea-wall. Although I was tempted to stop to rest on the great defensive barrier, I kept on flying until I reached Gwyddno Garanhir's tower, and flew in through the turret window.

As soon as she was changed back to herself, T.A. started hurling things. An earthenware jug whizzed past my ear, a mirror skimmed past at neck height like a demented frisbee, a twelve-stringed *crwth* smashed musically against the wall behind me, and the words she threw were almost as hard. I didn't know what to do except duck, and I did a lot of that. However, my temper was beginning to flare up, because my arms hurt, and my beak – sorry, my teeth – hurt, and I had saved her from a fate worse than death and now she was trying to kill me!

Then, Nest was flying in, and O'Liam, and as Nest changed back, her voice rang out. 'T.A., stop this at once.'

I'd never heard Nest's voice anything but soft, but now – well! It was enough to make T.A. meekly put down the pewter tankard she was about to hurl and burst into tears.

'You've ruined my life, you have,' she wailed. 'I didn't want to leave. Conor loves me. He says he can't live without me. And I love him, too!'

'Don't be ridiculous,' I snapped. 'That weasely, sneaky little leprechaun isn't capable of loving anyone. He's put a spell on you, that's what he's done.'

'He hasn't!' sobbed T.A. 'He loves me. You don't understaaaaand!'

'Oh, for goodness sake. Pull yourself together, T.A., you –'

'T.A.,' Nest interrupted calmly, 'if you really love Conor, then we shall take you back.'

I swung round and stared at her. 'We'll do what?'

'You heard what I said, Tansy. If she really loves Conor, then she can go back. But O'Liam knows Conor as well as anyone. He will know the truth. O'Liam?'

O'Liam was looking uncomfortable, even for a sparrow-hawk. I shifted him back and he shuffled his feet, stretched his arms and examined his fingers and feet, trying to get used to being a leprechaun again. Once he was confident that feathers weren't going to sprout from the seat of his breeches, he gazed at T.A. sorrowfully.

'I know Conor of the Land Beneath as well as I know myself, Lady Haf,' he sighed. 'And there is just one person he loves much more than any other person in the world at all, so.'

'Me,' T.A. said, confidently.

'No. It is Himself,' O'Liam said. 'To be sure, he's put a spell on you. I know the very enchantment he

136

has placed upon your head, I do so. Did he feed you honey, now?'

T.A. stared at him. Then, she slowly nodded.

'And did he feed you thick, thick cream?' The little man's Irish accent turned the word into 't'ick, t'ick'.

T.A. nodded.

'Did he tie you round and round with purple silken thread and make a game of it, with kisses and such?'

T.A. went pink.

'And when he untied you, did he kiss your lips three times, mwah, mwah, mwah, so?'

T.A. nodded, blushed and burst into tears. 'That doesn't mean he doesn't love me,' she sobbed, 'in his own way, I mean.'

O'Liam shook his head again. 'Believe me, Lady, Conor of the Land Beneath loves no one. He cannot. He does not know how.'

'He must have, once,' T.A. wailed. 'What about Maebh? Didn't he once love her?'

'He did, so,' O'Liam agreed. 'But when she left him she broke his heart and took the pieces of it with her to dance upon. And now he has no heart at all.'

'But I love him!' T.A. said again.

O'Liam nodded wisely. 'That will be the enchantment talking.'

'I don't know this spell,' I said. 'Nest, do you?'

The half-fairy shook her head. 'How can we take it off if we don't know it?'

'But I know it,' O'Liam said, 'and I can take it off. But first –'

Here it comes, I thought, *the leprechaun's bargain. Never trust a leprechaun, right?*

137

'First, thank you a thousand, million times for bringing me here. Conor would have killed me altogether dead as a doorstep for helping you, but you are my blood kin, Nest, and they say blood is thicker than porter. Also your Lady kindly saved me from the terrible giant. I will work for you for ever and *two* days!' he promised.

I felt a bit guilty at having misjudged him. 'Thank you, O'Liam. We o- 'I caught Nest's eye and hesitated. 'Thank you for opening the door for us,' I finished. I didn't feel confident enough in the leprechaun to owe him our lives just yet. 'Now, can you take off the spell?'

'I can, so.'

'What do you need?'

'I need a golden spoon, about so long, and a square piece of black silk, and some butter. Unsalted, mind,' he said sternly, raising his finger, 'and some fresh-baked crusty bread. And some honey. Oh. And some cow's milk. Warm from the beast.'

Nest went running to find Gwyddno Garanhir to tell him that we were back, and to get the stuff O'Liam had asked for. When it came, the golden spoon, the silken square, the milk in an earthenware jug, the honey, the rich yellow butter and bread still warm from the oven, we placed it on a table and watched as O'Liam sat T.A. down.

He made her open her mouth, and placed the handle of the golden spoon between her teeth, the bowl facing up and out. 'Don't, whatever you do, let it drop,' he ordered. 'Whatever happens, *keep hold of that spoon with the teeth that are in your mouth.*'

'Argle,' T.A. said, nodding furiously. It's hard to

speak while holding a spoon between your teeth, I suppose.

Then O'Liam tied the black silk around her eyes like a blindfold, and poured the milk in one steady stream over the top of it. Most of it ran off the ends of her hair and pooled in her lap, but some of it inevitably landed in the bowl of the spoon, and he said sternly, 'take care that you spill not a drop, now, or the spell will not work.'

T.A. almost nodded, but thought better of it just in time.

'Right, so,' O'Liam said. 'Very quickly, tip your head so that the milk that is in the spoon runs into your mouth. Keep your teeth tight clenched but your lips open, now.'

T.A. obediently jerked back her head. The milk ran down the handle and trickled into her mouth. O'Liam muttered a few words under his breath, carefully removed the spoon, untied the black silk and squeezed it out over T.A.'s head, and placed them both on the table.

'There,' he said, folding his arms. 'Now, Lady. Will you go back to the Land Beneath and Conor who says he loves you?'

'What?' T.A. said, and shuddered. 'That little creep? I'd rather poke myself in the eye with a sharp stick.'

I let out the breath that I had been holding. 'Oh, T.A., thank goodness you're back. Thanks, O'Liam. That's –' I was about to say 'one more we owe you' but thought better of it. Then I noticed the bread, honey and butter still on the table. 'Did you forget part of the spell?' I asked, worriedly.

The leprechaun looked indignant. 'I did not. The whole thing was done right and proper, it was indeed.'

'Then why the . . .?' I indicated the food still on the table.

O'Liam shifted his feet about and went pink. 'All that flying and spell-taking makes a person starving hungry, so it does. Can I offer you a piece of this good bread, now?'

I was so grateful I magicked him some Marmite to have on it as well. I like Marmite, OK?

O'Liam spread a little on his bread and butter and sniffed it suspiciously. 'With the sinister little black pot, and the nasty yellow label,' he said. 'Are you sure you're not trying to poison me?'

'Try it!' I urged.

He nibbled. An expression of pure delight spread over his face. Then, 'Do you know what? A little morsel of strawberry jam on the top would make the whole thing perfect!'

I shuddered. Marmite and jam? Ugh. But I magicked him some anyway. O'Liam liked it, we had T.A. back, we were safe, and we knew – more or less – where Gwydion was. At least, Nest did.

We spent the night with Gwyddno Garanhir, and flew out of his lowland country as the first pink streaks of dawn tinted the crystal rivers red as blood and turned the marble towers pink. As I flew past the tallest tower, I saw that it was filled with long, dangling strings of sea-shells that shifted and shivered in the sea-winds, making an eerie, tinkling music. I felt a cold chill that had nothing to do with the sea air.

16

It was quite a way back to the *tŷ hir* from the coast, but at last the longhouse appeared on the horizon. I heaved a great sigh of relief, longing for something hot to eat and a good night's sleep. But then, as we flew closer, something began to niggle at me, about the longhouse. I wasn't sure what it was, but there was *something*.

We landed, O'Liam's wings drooping with weariness, and Nest and I shifted back. She stepped forward to rap on the wooden door, but I caught her wrist and stopped her, putting a finger to my lips. 'Listen,' I whispered.

There was silence inside. It was too quiet altogether. I frowned. 'There's something wrong, Nest. Flissy should be here even if Iestyn is at Castell Du.' I'd already realised what had caught my attention: there had been no smoke drifting lazily from the hole in the thatched roof that served the *tŷ hir* as a chimney.

'Nest,' I whispered. 'I think it might be a good idea if –' Nest caught on straight away. She shifted back and led O'Liam and T.A. up into the branches of a nearby tree, where they perched and waited.

Now, I may be daft, but stupid I am not, so I changed into a black beetle and scuttled into the *tŷ hir* under the door. It was a bit difficult to see what was happening, what with all the rushes that were lying about on the earthen floor, and the fact that the sun was almost gone and the rushlights hadn't been lit, but

I struggled to the top of a stalk and looked around. At first, I thought the place was empty, but then my eyes picked out two shadowy shapes sitting in the corner. I climbed back down my stalk and went to look. If there had only been one of them, I wouldn't have had a clue who they were, but there were two: alike as peas in a pod, and I guessed immediately.

Imagine a person with thin, floppy gingery hair, eyes set much too close together, eyebrows that meet in the middle, a long pointed nose like a shrew, sticky-out ears, very few teeth, and what there are of them greenish-yellow. Then multiply it by two, and without a doubt you have the twin sons of Rhiryd Goch: Ardwyn and Jason. They even had identical drips on the ends of their pointy noses.

So where was Flissy? I decided the best thing to do was to hang about and listen. After a while, the one on the left spoke in a hoarse whisper.

'Jase, I'm cold.'

'Yeah. Me too.'

'We could light the fire.'

'We could. 'Cept we haven't got anything to light it with.'

'No.'

'Jase, I'm cold.'

'Yeah, me too.'

At this point I decided that they probably had half a brain cell each. If that.

'Ard, what we waiting for, anyway?'

'Because Rhiryd told us we had to.'

'Oh.'

'Why?'

142

'Because he said.'

'Oh.'

Jason frowned, and honestly, I could almost hear the very little wheels going round! 'If we don't know what we're waiting for, why don't we go home then?'

'Because Rhiryd said we had to wait until...'

'Until what?'

'Can't remember.'

'Ard?'

'Yeah?'

'Let's go home.'

Ardwyn thought about this for a while, and then made a decision. 'Yeah.'

I just had time to scuttle into the cow-byre to avoid being trodden on as they flung open the door and stamped away round the back of the longhouse. Their horses had been hidden in the trees, and as the sound of hoofbeats faded, Nest, O'Liam and T.A. swooped down. I suddenly remembered, when I noticed O'Liam eyeing me hungrily, that I was still a (rather tasty) black beetle and it was a long time since the leprechaun had eaten. I hastily shifted myself, and the others, back.

'Flissy isn't here, and Rhiryd Goch's two sons were waiting for us. Luckily they aren't terribly bright, and seemed to have completely forgotten what they were waiting for, so I think we're safe for tonight at least. What do you think?'

The half-fairy was looking worried. 'If Rhiryd told them to stay, he'll certainly send them back as soon as he sees them if he's anything like his father was. No, it wouldn't be safe to stay here tonight.'

I felt helpless. 'Then where, Nest? We can't go to Castell Du, or Castell y Ddraig. Maebh probably has control over both at the moment.'

'We'll go to the village.'

My heart sank. 'We don't have to stay with Sion ap Sion, do we?' I pleaded.

'Good gracious, no! I thought perhaps Mali and Dafydd.'

I grinned. 'Good idea. She owes us one, anyway, since we got her her heart's desire.'

We shifted again and flew there, landing outside the small cottage, shifted back and knocked on the door.

'*Pwy sy 'na?* Who is it?' Mali's voice, sounding a little nervous.

'Nest, Mali,' Nest said. The door opened, and Mali saw us and squeaked.

'Oh, Nest, and Lady Tan'ith, thank goodness you're back! There's dreadful things been happening all over the place since you've been gone. Come in, quick.'

We slipped into the cottage past her, and by the glow of the flickering rush-lights I saw that the rocking chair in the corner was empty. I felt sad at the thought that Mali's old, old mother was apparently no longer with her. Mali's husband, Dafydd, was sitting at a rough wooden table eating broth from a bowl. He glanced up as we entered, dropped his spoon and stood up.

'Oh, no, Mali! We can't have them here! If Rhiryd ap Rhiryd or that Henbane person finds out we'll be for it. Shoo, shoo!' he said, flapping his arms as if we were chickens. 'Go away.'

I think I must have been tired, because I lost my

temper. Poor little O'Liam was nearly dead on his feet with tiredness, and T.A. was tearful. But me? I was MAD.

I took a deep breath, drew myself up to my full five feet not-a-lot and scowled at him. 'How dare you, Dafydd? How do you dare to speak to the Lady of Ynys Haf like that? Do you know what I could do to you if I wanted?'

Mali promptly burst into tears and hurled herself at Dafydd's chest. 'No, Lady, don't frog him or toad him or anything, please, please. He don't mean it, he's only frightened, that's all.'

'And so he should be,' I thundered. 'Of ME! And of Gwydion Dragonking, when he returns to his throne.'

'They say Gwydion Dragonking is dead, Lady,' Dafydd mumbled. 'And Queen Maebh is our ruler now. You don't have no more power in Ynys Haf, Lady Tan'ith.'

'Do you,' I said menacingly, 'want to bet?' I raised my right hand and Mali squealed in terror.

'No, Lady, I don't want to be married to a frog and have millions and millions of tadpoles! Please, Lady, mercy!'

Nest, fortunately, because I was beginning to run out of steam, stepped in and spoke soothingly. 'It's all right, Dafydd. Lady Tan'ith won't harm you. All we want is a night's shelter and to know what has been happening since we've been away. And by the way,' she said, patting Mali's hiccupping back, 'Gwydion Dragonking isn't dead.'

Dafydd's face broke into a smile. 'Honest, Lady Nest?'

145

'Honest. We have found out where he is and will bring him back to Ynys Haf as soon as we can. Now, Mali, is there any of that good broth left to share with hungry people? My cousin O'Liam has travelled all the way from the Land of Finn MacCuill and he's exhausted.'

'Irish, is it?' Mali said, glancing at O'Liam. 'I had an aunty was Irish, once. Talked funny.'

'Did she, so?' O'Liam said, politely.

'Aye, she did! Just like that!' Mali said delightedly.

Mali, common-sense as restored as it ever would be, bustled about finding bowls and stools and spoons, and we gratefully sat around the table and ate the steaming broth. When we had finished, we pushed the bowls aside. O'Liam was falling asleep in his bowl, and so I magicked him a new, beautiful goosedown emerald sleeping bag with a shiny zip to replace the one he'd left in his quarters in the Land Beneath. We tucked him up in it with the zip closed under his pointy chin. He didn't so much as stir when Dafydd lifted him.

The rest of us sat about the fire, toasting our knees. 'Dafydd,' I said, 'what has been happening here while we've been away? Where is my aunt?'

'Oh, Lady Tan'ith,' he said mournfully, 'it has all been dreadful. Master Iestyn has been up at Castell Du the whole time, and he hasn't been back to the village not at all. He hasn't seen Lady Flissy, neither, and then his sister took sick and Lady Fliss had to go up to Castell Du to tell him all about it because he couldn't come to her.' He put his head in his hands and groaned.

'And?' I prompted.

'Well, it appears as how Queen Maebh can smell a witch. And as soon as Lady Fliss got through the gates of Castell Du, she smelled her and had her locked up in the dungeon. And she's there still, and they won't let Iestyn see her, neither.'

'What?' I said, stupidly, 'but there aren't any dungeons in Castell Du. Gwydion had them all filled in, didn't he?'

'Aye, he did, Lady. But that Henbane had them all dug out again. And nearly filled them up with people, too,' he said bitterly. 'Anyone who steps out of line, don't do what that Henbane orders, or can't pay his taxes – and great big fat taxes they are, too, Lady – poof. Straight in the dungeon, bread and water if they're lucky, shackled hand foot and finger.'

'But Flissy is a *witch*.' I didn't understand. 'Witches don't stay anywhere they don't want to stay. All she has to do is shape-shift and she's out of there.'

'Not if the dungeon is lapped and lined with iron, Lady.'

I stared at him. Iron. The one thing that can neutralise magic entirely. And if she was held in an iron cell, I couldn't get in to help her, either. Here in Ynys Haf iron has the same effect on me as it does on all witches. It zaps us, like Kryptonite zaps Superman.

'So you see, everything's gone wrong, Lady,' Mali said sadly. 'My old Mam flatly refused to pay the great big whopping tax that Henbane slapped on her chickens, even though we begged and pleaded with her so she'd give in. But no, and so he dragged her off and locked her up, too! And her four hundred and

147

ninety-five next birthday! She said there wasn't anyone she was paying taxes to except Gwydion Dragonking, and he was too nice and polite to ask for taxes from an old age pensioner, and Henbane could go and whistle for it. Truth is, she said something a bit ruder than that, Lady, but I can't repeat it in polite company. But Mam will be suffering with her achey joints and bones, and I don't know how to help her. And though you say the Dragonking isn't dead, I don't see him anywhere around rescuing us from the tyrant, do you?'

'Don't worry. He'll be back,' I said fiercely. 'Nest knows where he is and first thing tomorrow we'll go and get him. And then we'll free not only Flissy but your poor old Mam as well. Right, Nest? You know exactly where Gwydion is, don't you, Nest?'

'Well, yes. Yes, I do.'

Our eyelids were drooping, so Mali found us all bedding and a place to lie down, and with Dafydd on guard, we lay down and attempted to sleep. T.A., exhausted by love, temper-tantrums and flying, zonked out straight away, but Nest and I lay next to each other, horribly tired and aching all over, but rigid and wide-eyed, worrying about Gwydion and Flissy, and Mali's poor old Mam, and unable to sleep at all.

'Are you sure you know where Gwydion is, Nest?' I asked at last, 'really, really sure?'

There was a long, long silence.

'I hope so, Tansy. Oh, I hope so.'

148

17

I must have slept at last, because I woke up in with a stiff neck and gritty eyes.

Nest was already awake, and busily stirring a pot on the fire in the middle of the room. O'Liam was still snoring contentedly.

'Where're Dafydd and Mali?' I asked, yawning and stretching to get the kinks out of my bones.

'Dafydd is catching up on his sleep after standing guard over us all last night. Mali is working at Castell Du as a kitchen helper, which is a good thing because she can slip her mother a bit of food now and again when no one's looking. Poor old soul.'

'Would you like some breakfast? There's bread and apples and some of Mali's Mam's blackberry jam.'

I was starving, and Mali's Mam's jam was more-ish, to say the least, and T.A. tottered blearily over and helped me finish the earthenware pot-full. When O'Liam woke up he tried to stand up in his sleeping bag before his eyes were open, and promptly fell over. We picked him up and helped him climb out of it.

'Ah, Lady,' he said, delightedly. 'Sure, haven't you found me another one of them good things!' He picked up the bag and hugged it. 'Slept like a baby, I did, so, and who wouldn't in a dear contrapulation like this.'

I cut him some bread, found a new pot of jam on the shelf and passed him the butter to go between the two. The way he socked into the food, I hoped Mali's Mam had had a good year blackberrying! Between the three of us there wasn't much left.

149

When we'd eaten and cleared away, Nest and I sat down to talk about our next step.

'Oh, I wish Taliesin was here!' I moaned. 'He'd know what to do.'

Nest gave me an exasperated glare. 'Look, Tansy, you've got to stop waiting for someone else to sort out your problems. It isn't going to happen. You don't seem to realise. It's up to you. You are the Lady of Ynys Haf. In Gwydion's absence, you're in charge.'

I sighed. 'But – 'I began.

'But nothing. You know exactly what we have to do. We have to find Gwydion and free him, release Flissy and Mali's Mam and anyone else that Henbane and Maebh have shut up, and take back Ynys Haf. With or without Gwydion.'

'What do you mean, "with or without"?' I asked anxiously. 'I thought you said you knew where we could find him?'

'Well, I think I do,' Nest said. 'In fact the more I think about what the Hermit of Glendalough said, the more certain I am. But until we actually go and look for him, I can't be sure.'

I racked my brains, trying to remember his exact words. *'Where the flowers meet the toad, and the river meets the road, and the sky meets the sea and the wind blows free,'* I quoted. 'I wish these mystical types would talk in plain language occasionally.'

'Have you forgotten what else he said, Tansy?'

I tried to remember. 'Um, I think I probably have.'

'We asked whether Gwydion was in Your Time Wales or in Ynys Haf,' she reminded me.

'Oh yes. And he said –'

'Yes – and no!' Nest finished.

'Yes and no?' T.A. stared at us. 'I see what you mean about not talking plain language, Tanz. What on earth can he mean?'

Nest shrugged. 'I don't know. But I think I know what the other part means – *where the flowers meet the toad, and the river meets the road, and the sky meets the sea, and the wind blows free* – I'm pretty sure there's only one place that can be in Ynys Haf.'

When O'Liam had finished eating and had tugged on his green boots, we made our plans. I made them, in fact, because I was still smarting from what Nest had said about me being in charge. She was right, of course. The trouble is, there is still little old cowardly Tanith Williams under all this Lady of Ynys Haf stuff. Bringing the two halves of me together was a bit hard. One half wanted to find somewhere very safe to hide until it was all over, and the other half wanted to go right out and trash the bad guys.

'T.A.,' I decided, 'you stay here with O'Liam. You can go out for a walk if you want, but don't go far from the cottage. Nest and I will go to wherever this place is that she thinks the Hermit meant. And with any luck we'll be back – with Gwydion – before nightfall.'

O'Liam bowed deeply towards T.A., pointing the toe of his green boot elegantly. 'Oh, honoured I am, Lady. Shall we go west, or east, or north or south? Or all four together at once?'

'We'll wash up first,' T.A. said, trying not to grin. 'Then we'll go where the fancy takes us.'

'Aaah!' O'Liam closed his eyes. 'What a wonderful

way you have with the spoken word. "Where the fancy takes us". Doesn't that bring all sorts of amazing possibilities into the head?' He opened one eye and fixed it on T.A. 'Mind, I have a feeling in my bones that the name that you gave Lord Conor is not the name that your Mammy gave you.'

'And you'd be right,' I said. 'Her real name is Teleri-Angharad.'

O'Liam's face fell. 'Sure I'll never get my tongue round that. The name goes on longer than the Dubh Linn river. Perhaps I'd better stick to "Haf".'

T.A. patted the little man's shoulder. 'You can call me T.A.,' she said kindly. 'Come on, I'll wash and you dry. Then after we'll go for a walk.'

Nest and I went outside. 'Do we shift, or what?' I asked. 'I haven't got the faintest idea where we're going. Is it far?'

'Quite a way. It's close to the coast, so gulls might be best.'

We shifted into great black-backed gulls, our powerful dark wings lifting us out of the clearing in the woods where Mali and Dafydd's cottage squatted, and through the sky towards the coast.

Nest led us North, towards the tall mountains of Eryri, their mass spread out before us, the air becoming colder and colder as we flew over them. And then we were coming down and down over a dark wood stretching almost to the edge of the sea. A small village clustered on the banks of a river and Nest swooped down to perch on the thatched roof of one of the huts.

She craned her neck, her orange eyes darting

152

around her. Then she took off again, me at her wing-
tip, circled once and swept downstream to a place
where the river crossed the road. When she landed, she
looked around to make sure no one was watching,
shimmered and shifted. I did the same, and looked
around me.

'Is this it?' I asked.

'I think so. Look at the woods behind us, Tansy.'

I turned and looked. From the dark edge of the
wood, a sapphire carpet of bluebells seeped out
towards the river.

'Where the flowers meet the toad: with the river so
close I bet there are toads around somewhere.' As I
said the word, a Natterjack, his gaudy yellow stripe
gleaming in the sun, hopped obligingly across my foot
and into the bluebells. 'There,' I said, my hopes of
finding Gwydion rocketing upwards.

'And the road fords the river at the shallowest
point,' Nest said, 'and in that direction you can see the
sea . . .'

'Where the sky meets the sea,' I said, *'and the wind
blows free.* Well, it's certainly doing that.' It was cold,
too, and I pulled my jerkin collar up.

'The wind blows free is the only bit that worries
me,' the half-fairy said. 'Yes, right now it's blowing a
gale, but it doesn't always. So maybe this isn't the
exact place.'

My hopes and my heart plummeted into my boots. I
was more or less expecting Gwydion to be close
enough to see once we had solved the Hermit's riddle.
But he wasn't. 'There don't seem to be any caverns
about, Nest. Are you sure this is the place?'

'It has to be the right place. But I think if we try to work out what "neither in Your Time Wales or Ynys Haf" means it *might* help. Come on, *think*.'

I sat on a large boulder, put my head in my hands and concentrated. Nothing. Far off in the distance I heard a dog bark, and it reminded me of Fflur, my wolfhound. I missed her, and before I knew it my mind had wandered off the problem of the missing Gwydion and after Fflur. I hoped the kid next door was looking after her. He was pretty good and had never forgotten to feed her before. Fflur had followed me the first time I went home after visiting. I remembered how scared I had been, going back into the Door in Time to fetch her that first time. I grinned, remembering. I'd been terrified of getting stuck half-way, my head in My Time Wales and – 'Nest,' I said, 'I've got it. I think I know where Gwydion is!'

Nest stared at me. 'You do? Honestly?'

'Honestly. Think, Nest. Where is the only place where you aren't in Ynys Haf and you aren't in My Time Wales.'

'Oh, Tansy, I've been thinking and thinking. There isn't anywhere at all.'

'Oh yes there is, Nest!' I said, triumphantly. 'The Time Doors! Going from here back to my time it takes ages, but the other way it's instant. So, it has to be –'

She stared at me. 'Of course! *Of course!*'

'So, where is the nearest Door?'

She bit her lip and concentrated. 'Oh, I know there's one near here. But where? Tansy,' she said, prodding me in the ribs, 'you're the Lady. You can *feel* it. Listen to Ynys Haf. Where is it? Come *on*. Try!'

I tried to tune into the feeling of Ynys Haf. The birdsong grew louder, the sun seemed warmer, and the earth and sky seemed to buzz with life and welcoming warmth. Then the boulder I sat on gave me an electric shock.

I shot about a metre in the air, yelping with surprise. When I landed, I rubbed my rear end and stared at the boulder. 'It attacked me!' I said, crossly. 'That boulder attacked me!'

'It did?' Nest stared at me. 'Then – '

'The Time Door. The boulder must be part of it. Is there another one like it anywhere around? So that we can walk between them, I mean. There are usually two upright stones to go through, aren't there?'

We searched, but there wasn't anything, anywhere, remotely like it. 'Well,' I reasoned, 'if it isn't one of a pair, then the entrance must be somewhere very close.'

'Or –' Nest began, but I was there first.

'Underneath it!' I said, and bent down. 'Come on, Nest, help me roll it away.'

We puffed and panted and heaved, the half-fairy and I, but we couldn't even rock it in its bed.

I glared at it. 'Damn thing. It must weigh a ton. Or be about twenty feet down in the earth like a bit of buried Stonehenge. Or it's got a spell on it or something.' Then I realised what I'd said. 'Of course! If Gwydion is down there, then whoever put him there wouldn't have made him easy to find, right?' I sat down (next to the boulder this time – I valued my situpon!) and once again concentrated very hard on *feeling* Ynys Haf. Suddenly my right hand got very hot. Not hot-and-sweaty, like it did at the dentist or in maths exams, but hot as a hotplate. It didn't hurt, but it was so hot that I stared at it, almost expecting to see it glow. Then I cottoned on to what was expected of me, stretched out my arm and laid my red-hot hand on top of the boulder. The heat that I felt disappeared instantly, and as I watched, the boulder turned bright red, went back to grey, and *floated* up in the air. Then it shifted politely aside and set itself down again a little way away, revealing –

A large hole and a flight of steps leading down into the earth.

18

The hole yawned darkly at our feet, looking, as mysterious holes in the ground tend to do, a bit on the sinister side. I took a deep breath, gathered up all my courage (didn't take long – there isn't a lot of it!) and started down the steps. They curved and twisted, and the deeper we went the darker it got. Soon I was feeling my way along the walls, Nest behind me. I don't like being in the dark, especially when I don't know if the dark in question is spidery or not. Thinking about it though, spiders were probably the last things I needed to worry about. It was all very well being the Lady of Ynys Haf, and a Daughter of the Moon, but where was the moon when I needed it?

No sooner had the thought crossed my mind than a faint glow appeared in the air in front of me. It grew brighter and brighter until it was almost dazzling. I boggled. It was the moon, no doubt about it, I could see the familiar patterning on its surface – but in miniature. And what was it doing underground? Lighting your way, dingbat, my commonsense said.

We were in a long tunnel that seemed to stretch forever. Nest and I walked on, our eyes alert, our ears listening hard for any sounds or sights that might mean danger. Suddenly, I noticed a groove chiselled into the rocky ground in front of me. It went from one side of the tunnel to the other, up the wall, across the roof and down the other side. While I was wondering what it could possibly mean, I stepped across it and

157

rapidly found out! A mighty wind came from nowhere, and shoved me back, and I collided with Nest who hung on to me until I got my balance.

'Don't turn round, Tansy,' she warned, 'remember you are in a Time Door!'

If she hadn't warned me, I might have done just that. I knew that it was very dangerous to turn round in a Door in Time: that was one way to get permanently stuck there. I just wasn't expecting the wind, that's all.

'What was that?' I gasped.

'Some Doors have little booby-traps,' Nest replied, shoving me forward. 'Like the wind that blows you right back where you came from. If a bird flies in by mistake, it will blow it safely out again. It usually makes people turn round, instinctively, to shield their faces from the blast. We'll be all right if we just keep on pushing forward. And whatever you do, remember not to turn.'

'Where the wind blows free – this is it, Nest!'

I stepped forward again, into that massively strong wind that flattened my hair to my skull and felt as if it were trying to turn my face inside out. We staggered along, Nest pushing me from behind (and sneakily sheltering in my lee, as well!) for what seemed like miles. This must be the Door to our Time the long way round! And then, as suddenly as it had started, the wind dropped. Ahead of me there was a square opening with daylight showing.

'We're almost out in My Time!' I groaned. 'Gwydion can't be here after all.' I had been so sure that we'd find him. 'Oh, Nest, he's got to be here! It all fits, doesn't it?'

If I hadn't been so depressed that my head drooped, I might not have seen the marks in the ground. I knelt and looked closer. The mini-moon obligingly followed me, lighting up the shape of a large square. 'It's a trap-door!' I said. 'Maybe he's down here, Nest!'

Together we pulled and pushed and heaved (and all without turning round in the tunnel) and at last we got the trick of it and the trapdoor creaked and slid smooth as chocolate to one side. Another flight of steps led even further down into the rocks beneath the earth. 'Moon?' I said, hopefully, and it obligingly bobbed through the square opening ahead of me. More steps, winding round and round and down and down.

And then we were in a small cavern hewn out of the rock. The walls were damp and dark, and without the moon it would have been unbearable down here. A bed stood in the centre of the cavern, and on it lay a figure.

It was Gwydion, and he was snoring.

Nest and I swiftly crossed to the bedside, and I prodded him, hard. 'Come on, lazybones,' I said. 'Time to get up.'

He didn't move. I prodded him again, and still he didn't stir so much as an eyelash. At least he was breathing. 'Gwydion?' I said, uncertainly.

'He's under a spell, Tan'ith,' Nest said. 'Until we know what it is, we can't wake him.'

'Then how,' I asked crossly, 'are we supposed to get him out of here?'

'Shift him, of course,' she said. 'You aren't using your brain.'

She was right, of course. I gazed at the Dragonking

159

of Ynys Haf. His mouth was open and he didn't look in the slightest bit kingly.

Then my brain really got going. 'Nest,' I said slowly. 'We can't just shift him and take him out of here, remember? We can't even turn round in the Time Door – we certainly daren't shift an enchanted Gwydion! We shall have to carry him out into My Time, and then bring him back again.'

'Drat,' the half-fairy scowled. 'You're right, we can't shift him. That would scramble all his bits, and who knows what might happen? We'll have to take him through first, then turn round and bring him back into the Time Door.'

I stared at the (as far as I could tell, him being horizontal) six-foot-five lump on the bed, then looked at Nest. 'This is going to be fun, Nest,' I said. 'Not.'

'It might be easiest if we roll him off the bed onto the blanket thing he's covered with,' I suggested. 'Then we can sort of drag him along.'

So we put the coverlet on the floor beside the bed and rolled him off the bed and on to it. I took the head end and Nest took the foot. We shifted him about half a metre in ten minutes, and then I collapsed on the floor in a panting heap. 'This isn't going to work, Nest. We'll have to leave him and come back with a wheelbarrow or someone big and strong . . .'

And then I realised how totally and utterly dumb I was being. I couldn't shift Gwydion – but I could shift us! 'Nest, you aren't going to believe how stupid I am. Hang on.'

She made an amazing gorilla. A small one, but a gorilla with arms like small tree-trunks and a powerful back. I shifted myself and resisted the temptation to beat myself on the chest with my fists and bellow 'Oooooaaaraar!' Then we picked up the Dragonking as if he were a Tesco carrier bag and had him up those stairs like a rat up a drainpipe. We carried him to the opening of the Door in Time, shifted back to our ordinary weak selves, and tugged and heaved him through it.

We were standing halfway up a hillside somewhere, overlooking a town I didn't recognise. In the distance huge chimneys vomited black pollution into the sky, and the seas off the coast were brown and dirty. I had forgotten how much My Time stank after the pure air of Ynys Haf, and choked a little.

Then we dragged him towards the Door again, lifted him about half an inch (all we could manage) off the ground, and stepped back into the tunnel. The journey from My Time Wales into Ynys Haf is always instant: one minute I was in Wales, the next I was climbing out of the hole in the ground into the pure sea air of Ynys Haf. We dragged Gwydion's head out, changed him into a mouse, still fast asleep, and I laid him on the ground. Then I shifted into a very large raven and picked him up. I had to concentrate very hard, because there's nothing a raven likes better than a fat, juicy mouse. And I was hungry . . . It would be too bad if, after all we'd been through to find Gwydion, I forgot myself and sort of – swallowed! Nest shimmered and shifted beside me, and we flapped untidily into the air.

We headed back to Mali's cottage and swooped down and shifted ourselves. The cottage was empty, and I put Gwydion the mouse on the straw pallet that I had slept on the night before, and shifted him back. His feet were hanging off the end.

'Now, Nest,' I said, 'any ideas how we can break this enchantment? He's not a whole lot of use as a Dragonking in this condition.'

The half-fairy looked determined. 'We'll manage it somehow, Tansy. We'll work together on this. Oh, I wish I had my Physicians of Myddfai book, but it's back at the *tŷ hir*. I'll try to remember what's in it. You sit and concentrate very hard on the Lady's Magic. Oh, and the Emerald Spellorium, of course.'

That was the great thing. I had learned the Spellorium off by heart ages ago, and didn't need the book to remember. I also had all the Lady's bits and bobs of magic whizzing around inside me. So I went and sat in the corner with my fingers stuffed in my ears, muttering to myself, and Nest grabbed a handful of hair on each side of her face and concentrated, trying desperately to remember the hundreds of recipes and potions that are in the Physicians' Book.

While Gwydion snored.

I tried the *Spelle to Wayke a Sleeper That Hath beene Enchanted by a Faerie*. Gwydion snored on.

I tried the *Spelle to Wayke a Sleeper That Hath Fallen Foule of a Wittch*. Gwydion snored on.

I tried the *Spelle for Those That Knowe Knot Whatte Day Yt Is*. Gwydion snored on.

I tried the *Spelle for Those Whoose Boddies Thinke Thatte Yt is Night Whenne Yt Ys Daye*. Gwydion snored loudly on.

I tried the *Potion with Herbes and Hunny for the*

Rousing of Catatonics, that made me think of Catatonia and Cerys Matthews and how very little she needed rousing. Unlike Gwydion, who snored on.

I tried the *Resippe Ewsing Hotte Horseradish and Cowpatties Tied to Ye Feette.* That not only didn't work, it ponged something awful and made my eyes water.

Then Nest had a go. She tried the only one that the Physicians had to offer. Their cures were more for putting someone to sleep who was having difficulty in dropping off than waking someone who was overdoing it. She got some goose-feathers and set fire to them. Then she held the smouldering, smelly feathers under Gwydion's sleeping nose. He sneezed very loudly seven times. But he didn't wake up.

'That's it,' I said, in despair. 'There's nothing more we can do.' I gazed at Gwydion's sleeping body. 'Well, at least we've got him back, even if we can't wake him up. Oh, Nest, there must be something else we can try.'

Nest's small face was furious. 'Get hold of Henbane or Maebh and wring the spell out of them somehow.'

Since we couldn't even get near them without Maebh smelling our magic, fat chance. Besides, we were the good guys. We didn't use torture no matter how tempted we were, right? The sun had gone down while we had been working over Gwydion, and so I took a twig from the fire and lit the rush-lights. The flickering glow illuminated an emerald green sleeping bag in the corner.

'Nest,' I said suddenly, remembering, 'shouldn't T.A. and O'Liam be back by now?'

163

19

Nest's hands flew up to cover her mouth. 'They went out, didn't they?'

'But they wouldn't stay out, not this late. It's getting dark, and T.A.'s got more sense,' I said. 'So where are they?'

At that moment the latch lifted and Mali came in, closely followed by Dafydd. She flopped onto the bench and kicked off her wooden shoes. 'Oh, there's a day,' she moaned. 'If one more of those soldiers had pinched my –' she saw Dafydd's frown and stopped. 'Well, never mind. Oh, lovely to sit down!' She spotted Gwydion. 'Ooh! Look! It's Gwydion Dragonking, fast asleep on our bed, ooh, look, Dafydd! There's an honour.' She fidgeted about as if she were wondering whether she ought to curtsey, but then she saw the expression on Nest's face. 'What's the matter with him?'

'He's asleep. Don't worry, I'm sure he'll be fine,' Nest said. 'It's just that we're worried about Haf and the lepr – O'Liam. They went out for a walk and aren't back yet.'

Dafydd looked concerned. 'They ought to be back by now, Lady. Not safe out there at night. Not with that Henbane about. Great one for scooping up people and sticking them in his dungeons, Henbane is.'

'I think,' I said slowly, 'that we'd better go and look for them, Nest.'

'Shall I go?' Dafydd offered. 'You ladies shouldn't be wandering about in the dark by yourselves either.'

'You forget, Dafydd,' I said, shifting into a handsome snowy owl, 'I'm a witch,' I squawked. Nest swiftly changed, and we blinked up at Mali and Dafydd. Mali hid her eyes behind her hand, totally unnerved, and Dafydd stared. Of course, he'd never seen us change before. He opened the door – extremely rapidly – and we flew out.

I loved being an owl. It had been one of the very first shifts I made, and there was something about the absolute silence of owl-flight, the keenness of owl-sight in the darkness, and the feel of wind through soft white feathers, that was completely wonderful. But we were searching for our friends who were lost, and there was little time to enjoy it.

First we swooped and circled over Castell Du, and then side-slipped in to perch on the battlements well away from the tower where Maebh had her apartments. I hoped we should see Iestyn, and we sat silently side by side watching and waiting. After a long time, when my claws were beginning to stiffen from clutching cold stone, I saw him come out of the Great Hall and walk across the courtyard. Leaving Nest to keep watch, I flew low over his head to attract his attention and perched on a torch-bracket on the wall, careful to avoid the flickering flames. When I was certain I had caught his eye, I slipped behind a small wall, waited until he followed me in, and shifted.

'Lady, you shouldn't be here,' he hissed. 'It's too dangerous.' He looked haggard and worried. 'Henbane has already taken my Flissy and locked her up in an iron dungeon. If he captures you and locks you up, too, Ynys Haf will never be free of him. You are the Lady, and magic, but even you couldn't escape from a room lined with iron.'

'Iestyn, listen, I haven't got long – Maebh will notice my magic if I hang around,' I whispered. 'T.A. and O'Liam have disappeared. Are they here? Has Henbane shoved them in a smelly dungeon somewhere?'

He looked mystified. 'No, Lady. I'm sure I would have heard. News travels fast here. I knew within ten minutes that he had Flissy,' he said bitterly. 'What I don't know is why she risked coming here.'

I opened my mouth to tell him that his sister had been taken ill, which was why Flissy had come to Castell Du, to tell him, but then I shut it again. Iestyn had enough to worry about. As soon as Nest and I had found T.A. and O'Liam, we would find Iestyn's sister and cure her. I was sure we could do that, even if we couldn't wake Gwydion.

'If they aren't here, then where are they?' I wondered aloud.

Iestyn frowned. 'Maybe that leprechaun isn't to be trusted, Lady. He's one of the Little People, after all. It's a well known fact that leprechauns are untrustworthy and downright sneaky. Perhaps he's taken her somewhere and –'

'I'm sure you're wrong,' I said firmly. Even though I was learning all about leprechauns and their (fairly dishonest) little ways, somehow I trusted O'Liam. He was almost family, and he had saved our lives. 'O'Liam is for us, Iestyn,' I said firmly. 'He would never harm T.A., I'm sure of it. And if they aren't here, then they are somewhere else and we must go and find them.' I shifted back and rejoined Nest on her wall and told her what Iestyn had said.

'If they aren't here,' she said grimly, 'then where are they? Either they are lost or someone has them.'

So we took to the skies again, and flew great searching loops around the castle, swooped through the woods around Mali's cottage, our great owl eyes missing nothing. We made wider and wider circles, further and further afield, but there was no sign of T.A. and the leprechaun. We went higher, up towards the mountains, and searched the foothills, but there was still no trace. It wasn't until we had all but given up hope of ever finding them, and were heading disconsolately back towards Mali and Dafydd's hut when we spotted the glow of a small fire tucked secretly away in a fold in the rocks on the seaward side of Castell Du.

They were tied hand and foot. T.A. was red-faced with fury and struggling to get free, but O'Liam lay still as a stone, his face ghostly in the darkness, only the whites of his panicky eyes showing that he was still alive.

A man sat next to the fire, roasting a rabbit on a spit. I remembered how long it had been since I had eaten and my beak watered. I spread my wings and slipped closer, still behind the stranger, out of sight.

When I could see him properly, I saw that he was unusually small, only the size of a little boy – or a leprechaun. And then he spoke and his accent confirmed it.

'Oh, now, O'Liam of the Green Boots,' he said

mockingly, 'you should be honoured, you should so. For didn't Conor of the Land Beneath send me personally to invite you back? He wants, he says, to reward you for being so helpful and all with the Lady. He had such plans for her, and for the dark one lying beside you also, her with the bad temper and the rude vocabulary. But his plans did not include her escaping, you know. Not at all. If it was up to me, then I should kill you here, squealing like the treacherous little pig that you are, but Lord Conor wants you back with all your wee bits and pieces intact.'

O'Liam blinked, but did not stir. T.A., though, redoubled her efforts and got madder and redder.

'When I left the Conor,' the leprechaun said mockingly, 'wasn't he telling me what he had in mind? Very inventive, he was being, so. "Shaun," he said, "you know the land across the Middlesome Sea as well as any man," and he was right, for haven't I spent half my whole life gathering little wee raggedy bits of information here and there in Innish Haff.'

Spy! I thought angrily.

'So who better to come and fetch you back, O'Liam, eh? Mind, it is certain that the Luck is with me, for didn't I find you *and* the bad-tempered one into the bargain? Oh, his Lordship will be grateful, he will indeed.' The leprechaun lifted the carcass of the rabbit off the flames and began to tear it apart, shoving great lumps of steaming meat into his mouth. O'Liam, whose mouth by rights should have been watering, knowing his appetite, gazed sightlessly up at the sky. A large tear formed in the corner of his eye, glistening in the firelight, and trickled down his neck.

That did it. I was so mad I leapt off my rock, shifting as I went, and almost gave T.A. a heart attack as I landed next to her. The leprechaun dropped the rabbit and overbalanced backwards in shock, and before he could recover himself I turned him into a slug. I bent down and glared at the nasty, black, slimy thing.

'Listen to me, you nasty little spy,' I said, 'I'm going to send you back to Conor the Creep with a message. If he sends any more spies to Ynys Haf, or makes any attempt to interfere with us in any way, there'll be trouble, you hear me?'

The slug, with difficulty (not having much of a neck) nodded. I most certainly had his entire attention.

Nest shifted. 'Tansy,' she said, mildly, 'are you intending to send him back to Conor in that shape? Because if you are, he won't get back for about ten years, the speed slugs travel. And there's the sea to consider. Slugs don't swim all that well.'

I grinned. 'No,' I said. 'I'm not going to let him go under his own steam. I'm going to post him.'

T.A. made an exasperated noise behind her gag, and I hurriedly untied her while Nest released O'Liam and grabbed him to stop him stamping on Shaun the Slug.

'You can't post him, Tanz,' she said, 'they haven't invented the Post Office yet.'

'Not the Post Office, no,' I said, and grinned. 'But pigeon post . . .' I turned the slug into a pigeon and held him very tight by his feet while I magicked a very rude note to Conor of the Land Beneath and fastened it to his skinny red leg. Then I tossed the bird into the air. The leprechaun/pigeon staggered around a bit until he got the feel of flying, then wheeled over our heads and flapped furiously in the general direction of his homeland.

'And if you know what's good for you,' O'Liam yelled after it, shaking his fist, 'you won't come near me ever again. If you hadn't crept up on me like a coward, Shaun of the Furtive Toes, you'd not have caught us at all, you would not, so!'

When the pigeon had disappeared in the darkness (and although he might not enjoy flying at night I was pretty sure he'd keep right on going anyway) O'Liam clutched my hand and kissed it very hard. 'Oooh, Lady, wasn't I thinking my last hour was upon me entirely. King Conor would have chopped me in cutlets and fried me for breakfast. And worse,' he said, shuddering. 'Lady, I owe you more than I can ever repay.' He started to look worried. 'There, and haven't I promised already I'd work for you forever and two days, so,' he said. 'What more can I promise?'

'Nothing, O'Liam,' I said, gently, 'you don't owe us anything. Why, we owe you our –'

'Oh, Lady, don't say it,' O'Liam moaned. 'Please don't.'

I stopped and stared at him. 'Why not, O'Liam?'

'Because I am a leprechaun, Lady, and there's an old saying that a leprechaun cannot change its spots.'

'I think that's "leopard" O'Liam,' I said. 'Leprechauns don't have spots. And besides, you are our friend, and Nest's cousin.'

'Still, Lady, please don't go saying those words.' The little man bent mournfully over the roasted rabbit. 'Ah, will you look at the quality of the dirt on that thing. And here's my stomach thinking my throat is cut entirely.'

170

'O'Liam,' I said, giving him a hug. 'When we get back to Mali's place you shall have the best dinner you've ever eaten in your whole life, I promise.'

And so I shifted them, and Nest and I led the way back to Mali's place.

What with all the excitement, I had completely forgotten to mention to T.A. that Gwydion was back, so when she walked through the door of the hut and saw him flat on his back and snoring she squeaked in amazement and bounced up and down excitedly.

'You found him!' she yelled happily. 'Gwydion, we're home!'

Gwydion, of course, carried right on snoring.

'Oh,' she said. 'He's back but he isn't, is that it?'

I nodded, sadly. 'We've tried just about everything, T.A. Still, there's always tomorrow. But first, food.'

We ate until we were stuffed, and O'Liam's little tummy was as fat and round as a beach ball. Added to the Big Macs was pizza-with-everything-but-the-kitchen-sink on it, and strawberries and cream and milk-shakes and coke and you-name-it, he ate it. He sat at the table too full to move, and gazed at Gwydion and burped politely behind his hand.

'Sure and he's a fine fellow,' he said admiringly. 'Will you look at the whole length of him there! Tall as a tree even if he's horizontally inclined, so. Mind, handsome isn't as handsome doesn't, and he doesn't appear to be doing much at all.'

I gazed at Gwydion sadly. At least we had him back, even if he was unconscious. Maybe an idea would come to me tomorrow.

'What happened to you two?' I asked T.A. 'How

171

did that sneaky little bloke manage to get the drop on you?'

O'Liam looked embarrassed. 'Oh, it was my fault entirely, Lady. Wasn't I telling T.A. all about my childhood in the Land Beneath and making her laugh? My attention was all over the place to be sure, Lady, and the nasty wee mouse-dropping had us in a twinkling, what with the sneaky, untrustworthy feet upon him. Used a net, he did, so. And my beautiful boots are gone also.' He gazed sadly down at his garish socks, which now had holes in the soles as well as both toes and the heels.

'Oh, O'Liam, not your beautiful green boots,' I said.

'And wasn't the nasty wee thing tickling my toes and making me squeal?' And without my beautiful boots the entire world will be calling me "O'Liam of the Ragged Socks" from this day forth to all time,' he said mournfully.

'No, they won't,' I said. I muttered a couple of words and with a discreet puff of smoke first the holey socks disappeared and were replaced by glittery red lurex ones, then a magnificent pair of green velvet slippers embroidered with gold thread went on top. To finish it off, I sent in a cloud of silvery smoke and when it cleared, on the bench beside the leprechaun stood the most wonderfully elegant pair of soft, emerald green leather boots with tasteful embroidery around the tops. He was quite overcome.

'Oh, Lady,' was all he could say. 'Oh, Lady.'

Dim problem, O'Liam,' I said. 'Now, apparently we can't wake Gwydion up right now this minute, but

we're working on that. However, there are other things
I've got to do – like get poor Flissy and Mali's Mam
out of Castell Du. The trouble is that damn iron-lined
dungeon. There's no way around that at all, for a
witch. And you'd have trouble, too, wouldn't you,
Nest? Fairies have problems with iron, too.'

The half-fairy nodded, sadly. 'And leprechauns are
magic beings, so O'Liam can't help us, either.'

The leprechaun stared from Nest to me and back
again. 'Iron, you say?' he said. 'Trouble with iron?'
He started to chuckle, and then giggle, and then laugh,
so hard that he fell off the bench and lay on his back,
kicking his legs in the air like a stranded beetle, the
gorgeous velvet slippers glinting in the firelight.
Exasperatedly, we stared at him. At last the laughter
died down.

'Have you quite finished, O'Liam?' I enquired.

'I have, so,' he said, wiping his eyes. 'But I am the
one leprechaun, Lady, who has no fear at all of iron.
Haven't I found the way round it?'

'You have?'

'Oh, Lady, that I have!'

20

All of us stared at the leprechaun as he produced an enormous purple hankie with green spots from his pocket and used it to wipe tears of laughter from his eyes.

'Right,' I said, sternly, 'explain.'

'Would there be any more of that wholly amazing cold stuff left, by any chance?' O'Liam said hopefully, and I magicked him a third chocolate ice-cream.

'But talk while you're eating, O'Liam, right?' I commanded.

'Well, it's a sin to do it, for doesn't this stuff require my entire attention, but perhaps you don't know, Lady, that there are different sorts of leprechauns. I am a leprechaun from the Land Beneath. There are also tree leprechauns – not to be trusted at all, if you'll take my advice, and there are river leprechauns that are doubly untrustworthy being slippery and wetsome, and there are the leprechauns that live close beside the ocean in caves, and *nobody* trusts *them*, and they tell me that there is a great land across the sea where there are more leprechauns than there are at home, having ee-migrated on boats and –'

'Yes, O'Liam, I think we get the general idea,' I said wearily. 'But tell me about you and iron. Please?'

'Sorry, Lady. Well, the Land Beneath is under the earth, so.'

'It is.'

'And didn't the One that made the Land Beneath fill

174

the earth with all sorts of stuff? And each Land Beneath leprechaun has his own speciality. Some hunt diamonds, some hunt moles for waistcoats, or earthworms to air out the dwellings, or rabbits for dinner, or underground springs to drink from, or great crystal caverns to make palaces in. You get the idea. Each to his own. And I,' he tapped himself on the chest with the hand holding the long sundae spoon, 'I am O'Liam the Valiant, Ironfinder. As well as being O'Liam of the Green Boots, which is in the way of being a nickname.'

'Do you mean,' I said, slowly, 'that you can not only find iron but deal with it, too?'

'Oh, I can indeed. You see,' he shovelled in a large spoonful of ice-cream and closed his eyes ecstatically, 'oh, this stuff, this stuff. You see, Lady, iron is only a mineral, and I have learned that if you address a mineral with respect, it will do as you say. Once it gets acquainted with great heat, mind, doesn't it get entirely above itself, but before it gets over-heated and over-excited, and sometimes afterwards also, iron is no trouble to me at all.'

'But Flissy is in an iron dungeon. Which means that the stuff is proper iron – whatdoyoucallit – smelted, right? So can you do anything with that?'

'Depends.'

I glared at him. 'On what, O'Liam?'

'On whether I can get at it. If there is a door to the dungeon, then I can open it. If there is a roof which is bare to the elements, then I can get through it. If there are walls on the outside, even if the whole is made entirely of iron, then I can get through. I sort of appeal to its better nature.'

'Iron has a better nature? No, on second thoughts I don't think I want to know. You might be able to get through. But can Flissy?' I asked.

'If I make a hole, of course she can.'

'And you can make a hole in an iron dungeon.'

'I can so. But first you must get me inside the Castle. And if Maebh can smell a witch's magic, she will surely be able to smell mine also. So before I can help get your Aunt out of the dungeon, you must first get me into it.'

I stared at Nest.

'It's impossible,' she said. 'Maebh will sense that we are there as soon as we put a foot inside Castell Du.'

'Unless she isn't there,' I said, slowly. 'If we can get Maebh – and Henbane of course – to be elsewhere when we try to get in, then we have a chance.'

'But how, Tansy?'

T.A. collected the bowls we had been eating from, all except O'Liam's, who hung on to his, perhaps in hopes of a refill. She was frowning. 'So, all we have to do is get Maebh and this Henbane bloke away from Castell Du and you and Nest and O'Liam can get in, right?'

I nodded.

'How about setting fire to it?'

'Oh, great idea, T.A.!' I said. 'And after, we can bury what's left of all the prisoners after they've been barbecued, right?'

'Oh. Right. Hadn't thought of that,' she said, and went and dumped the bowls in the water-trough just inside the front door.

'But I think you're on the right track. If we can

176

create a diversion somehow,' I said slowly, 'and lure them away from Castell Du, then while they are gone – we can get in.'

'Excuse me, Lady,' Dafydd went bright red. 'I think I've got an idea.'

'Let's have it then, Dafydd,' I said. 'All suggestions gratefully received.'

'Well, if you want a diversion there's always fire, as T.A. said, but that's a bit sort of drastic. But if it was a distraction – not necessarily fire – somewhere else, that would draw them away from the Castle, like.'

'I'm with you, Dafydd!' I said excitedly. 'In fact, I think I'm ahead of you. Henbane and Maebh wouldn't both come out of Castell Du if there was just a fire someplace, would they? But if they were invited somewhere special, they'd go for certain. Especially,' I said, grinning, 'if Maebh could dress up.'

'How about asking Gwyddno to invite them over?' Nest suggested. 'Good neighbours and all that?'

'Gwyddno Garanhir?' I stared at her. 'Do you think he'd do it?'

'Of course. He was Gwydion's father's greatest friend. If it's to help Gwydion, of course he'd do it. I'll go and set it up, you try and work out some way to get Gwydion back on his feet.'

We all turned and stared at the sleeping figure on the bed. 'Do you suppose he needs feeding?' I asked.

Nest shook her head. 'No. Enchantments like this suspend the body's needs completely. He'll just lie there –'

'Like two yards of felled tree,' T.A. contributed helpfully.

177

'– until you can find the right spell to remove the enchantment.'

I sighed. Then I had another thought. 'I was watching one of those telly documentaries – never mind, Nest, next time you're in My Time I'll show you a T.V. set and then you'll understand – about a hospital and there was this bloke in a coma. The doctor said that as well as turning him and washing him and feeding him, the nurses always talked to him, because hearing is always the last sense to go. Perhaps we should try talking him out of it.'

Nest looked unconvinced. 'Well, it won't do any harm I suppose. But I don't honestly think it will do any good.'

So Nest had a quick sandwich and a hot drink, shape-shifted, and then set off for Cantre'r Gwaelod to talk to Gwyddno Garanhir. T.A. and I took it in turns to have long conversations with Gwydion, which he totally ignored, while O'Liam curled up contentedly in his sleeping bag like a hamster and caught up on some sleep.

My voice was getting hoarse, and T.A. was holding her head trying to think of something intelligent to say, when O'Liam woke up.

'Are you still talking the poor boy's earses off?' he enquired. 'Sure and you two'd talk the hind legs off a Donegal donkey, you would so.'

'If there's a chance he can hear us, we've got to try,' I said indignantly, 'and he's not a poor boy, O'Liam, he's Dragonking.'

'Dragonking he may be,' the leprechaun said sadly, 'but right now he's about as kingly as a dormouse.

Here, you go and rustle up something to eat – something with them nice golden chippity things in it for preference – and I'll give it a go.'

The little man perched cross-legged on the end of Gwydion's bed and put his head on one side. 'Dragonking you may be, but don't you know it's entirely rude to snore when someone's trying to have an intelligent conversation with yourself? By the Seven Burbling Bogs of Tralee, take an interest, your honour.' O'Liam sniffed, happily. 'Ah, can't you just smell them chippity potato things? Now, what to talk about. Anything at all, I suppose, given it's kindly meant. As they say in the Land Beneath, *Níor bhris focal maith fiacail riamh,*' he said softly. 'Sure, "a kind word never broke anyone's mouth".'

Then he fell off the bed.

21

I heard the thump as O'Liam hit the floor and turned round. 'What's the matter?'

O'Liam's face was startled and his mouth was open. He shut it, quickly, and scrambled to his feet. 'Wasn't I chattering away to him and passing the time of day politely and before I knew it he moved. Not much of a move, mind, just a little sort of twitch.'

I stared at Gwydion. He wasn't moving now. 'Are you sure?'

'Do you think I'm mad altogether? Of course I'm sure.'

I bent over the bed and prodded Gwydion in the ribs. 'Gwyd? If you can hear me, blink. Or nod. Stick your tongue out. Waggle your foot or your finger. Anything. Please?'

But he lay as if he had been carved from wood. Always supposing wood could snore. I sighed. 'Well, if you're right, O'Liam, and he moved, he's obviously exhausted himself with the effort. What did you say to him?'

O'Liam ran his fingers through his golden hair and it stuck up like a wren's tail. 'I can't remember, Lady. Something entirely inconsequential, I expect, seeing as I've never been introduced to the lad. I don't have the littlest idea what like we'd have in common to discuss. It was just an old saying from the Land Beneath.'

I already knew how O'Liam mangled old sayings. It could have been anything.

T.A. was standing on the opposite side of the bed.

'Tanz,' she said, slowly, 'you don't think maybe it wasn't so much what O'Liam said as the way he said it?'

'What do you mean?'

'Well, maybe he was responding to the Irish accent rather than what O'Liam said?'

I shrugged. 'Aaah, we'll probably never know. Anyway, once we've eaten, what I've got to do is try again to find a spell that will bring him round. There must be *something* . . .'

'Now, would those big stripey sacks of food be for me?' piped up O'Liam.

'Us,' T.A. and I said together, firmly. There was no doubt O'Liam would eat the lot if he wasn't watched. After we'd eaten and I'd vanished the Kentucky Fried cartons, complete with clean-picked chicken-bones, I sat down at the table and started going through the Spellorium in my head once again.

I tried everything that seemed remotely useful. I raided Mali's dried herb supply dangling from the rafters (the herbs, not me), trotted outside in search of mouse-ear, (plant, don't worry) house-leeks, earthworms and onions, but nothing I tried worked. One problem was, although I had the recipes, sometimes I couldn't actually identify the plant. I mean, would you know what Aqua Benedicta Rulanda looked like? Or Petilla? Stibium? Melilot? Exactly. I didn't, either. And some of the recipes involved following various four-legged creatures around with little bottles trying to catch their – well, I won't go into that. But nothing I tried worked.

I was scratching my head trying without success to

think of something else, when the door of the hut crashed open and Mali hurtled in.

'Oooh, Lady,' she wailed, wringing her hands as if she were trying to separate bone from flesh, 'something terrible's happened! Oh, oh,' she shrieked, burying her face in her hands, 'you've got to do something, Lady, please!'

'Calm down, Mali,' I said, putting my arm round her comfortingly. 'I can't help if you don't tell me what's wrong, can I?'

'It's that Master Henbane,' she sobbed, 'he's gone and took my Dafydd and all the village elders and thrown them in his dungeons!'

'What, all of them? What for?'

'They couldn't pay their taxes, Lady, and he says he's going to keep them locked up until they die if they don't pay. How can we pay great big taxes like that? We haven't got any money left, and he's had all our livestock already. Oh, oh, Lady, we got to get my Dafydd out. He can't stand being shut up, he'll die for sure in there.'

I patted her hand, reassuringly. 'Don't worry, Mali, we'll rescue him. We've got a plan, honest.'

Mali cried most of the evening and finally tottered up the ladder to the sleeping loft and cried some more before falling asleep. O'Liam slithered with a contented sigh into his green bag and zipped himself up like a caterpillar larva, but T.A. sat up with me and waited for Nest. She flew in at about four in the morning, judging by the way the moon was drifting across the sky, and woke me from a half-drowse by lifting the latch on the cottage door.

'Nest, you're back. What happened?'

The half-fairy was white with tiredness and I hurried to get her something to eat and drink. 'I saw Gwyddno Garanhir and brought him up to date with what has been happening since we were last there. He was planning a feast anyway, something to do with the equinox, I think, and has agreed to invite Maebh and Henbane to it and keep them there as long as he can.'

'Perhaps we could just get him to lock them up in his dungeons for a while, until we've got Ynys Haf properly sorted,' I said.

'He wouldn't do that,' Nest said. 'He'll help us all he can, but he won't lock them up. He doesn't believe in it.'

'So, when's the rave-up?' I asked.

'Next weekend. I brought the invitation back with me, and delivered it in person to the gates of Castell Du – in disguise, of course! I imagine that Maebh and Henbane are already deciding what they're going to wear.'

'Let me think,' I sat at the table and tried to work it out. 'They'll have to leave very early Friday morning for them to reach Cantre'r Gwaelod in good time for a feast on Saturday. Today's Tuesday, so if we wait until Friday at noon –'

'Sun-top,' O'Liam said, who had woken up at the rattle of the bread-crock.

'Noon,' I corrected him, scowling at the interruption, 'then we can get into the castle, O'Liam can get Flissy out of the dungeon, we can rescue the others and Bob's your uncle.'

'No, there I believe you're wrong entirely,' O'Liam

said. 'I don't have an uncle by that name, not at all. I have an uncle Seamus, and an uncle McGill, and cousins Regan and Boylan, but –'

'That's just a saying, O'Liam,' T.A. said patiently. 'Tanz didn't mean that you actually have an uncle called Bob.'

The little man sighed. 'It's a strange, outlandish tongue you have to be sure.'

It was all very well saying that we'd wait until Friday noon, but the waiting was awful. If you know anything about me you'll know that (a) bravery isn't my best point, (b) waiting isn't either, and (c) if I've got to do something nasty I'd rather get it over with. And I had a feeling that this might be quite nasty.

But Friday noon (all right, O'Liam, Friday sun-top) finally arrived and I shifted T.A. and O'Liam into ravens before shifting myself, ready to fly to the castle, leaving Nest behind to take care of Gwydion. I would have felt happier if Nest had been with me, but it wasn't fair to leave T.A. behind. She didn't have any powers and would be helpless if anything went wrong. At least if she came with us I could keep an eye on her.

We flapped up into the clouds, pushing through the white mist into the blue above. The countryside below us unrolled like a carpet as we skimmed along on the back of the wind, heading for where the great black battlements loomed over the wild sea-coast of Ynys Haf. T.A. was showing off a little, doing loops and rolls, but when we got close to the castle I squawked at her to behave and pay attention. We circled once over the castle courtyard, and then swooped down.

Immediately, my heart sank. I'd expected that when Maebh and Henbane had gone to their feast they'd have taken Rhiryd, Jason and Ardwyn with them, but they hadn't. At least, they hadn't taken the twins. They were sitting on upturned barrels in the courtyard, eating apples.

Jason chomped his way through his apple and then hurled the core at the three ravens sitting on the battlements. He missed by a mile, but I bristled anyway, and opened my wings, cawing threateningly. Ooh, I'd get him sooner or later, the nasty little creep. O'Liam looked over his shoulder and watched the apple core shatter on the rocks beneath. I could tell he was thinking about food again.

'O'Liam,' I croaked, 'you do your bit this afternoon and get Flissy out of the iron dungeon, and I'll feed you until you can't move at all, I promise. But first we have to find her.'

'Here, Ardwyn,' Jason said suddenly, squinting at us. 'See them ravens up there?'

Ardwyn glanced up and nodded.

'If I had my crossbow, I could pick them off one after the other, just like that.' And he put a pretend crossbow to his shoulder and went 'Ping, ping, ping'.

'So you say.'

'Could!'

'Couldn't!'

'Could! Ping, I'd go, ping, ping, and that would be the end of them.'

Ardwyn was watching us now. 'Jase,' he said suddenly, 'them three ravens. Isn't there supposed to be a law against three ravens?'

185

'A law?' Jason was obviously confused. 'How do you mean, a law?'

'Well, not a law exactly. But don't it mean bad luck?'

'Superstitious rubbish,' Jason said. 'Ravens aren't bad luck. Albatrosses, now, you pop off at one of them and all sorts of bad things happen.'

'Oh.'

'Jase,' Ardwyn said after a while. 'What's an Albert Rossy?'

I decided we'd had enough of this conversation and dropped backwards off the wall, closely followed by O'Liam and T.A. I swooped downwards to the beach below the castle and landed on the jagged rocks.

'How are we going to find Flissy, Tanz?' T.A. squawked.

'I think what I shall have to do is fly round the base of the castle and hope I can feel the iron through the walls. I've never felt it, but I know it's supposed to have an effect on me. I expect I'll recognise it when I feel it.'

O'Liam put his head on one side and gazed at me, his bright black eyes glinting over the heavy beak. 'Oh, you will that, Lady,' he said. 'Soon as you get within range of iron you'll fall out of the sky, that's what you'll do.'

'You're joking!'

'I am not. But what with me being on the small side, many a true word is spoken to the chest. Don't you understand, Lady? Iron is the greatest threat to your kind. It takes your powers away, phoot! No magic.'

I drooped my head, pecking thoughtfully at one inky foot. The bird equivalent of biting my fingernails, I think. 'So, what are we going to do?'

'Sure, and I'd have thought it entirely obvious. I shall find the iron. That's what I've trained my whole life for, is it not? Finding iron. And when I find it I shall come back and tell you where it is.'

'And then I can go with you and – oh no, I can't, can I?'

O'Liam shook his raven's head. 'You cannot, Lady. But I will find your aunty and get her out of the dungeon if I can. And then maybe I can talk the iron into behaving itself and letting you get near it to help free the other prisoners.'

'I could go with you though, couldn't I?' T.A. said. 'I'm not a witch.'

'That's true indeed,' O'Liam said, 'but you borrowed a witch's magic and once you get near the iron –'

'Phoot?'

'Phoot,' O'Liam agreed. 'So now, Lady. This is where I begin to repay the great debt I owe you.' And the raven took off, rode an up-thermal to the top of the cliffs, and began to fly around the castle.

22

Although it was late spring, it was a bit on the chilly side, hanging around on the sand like that. T.A. and I fluffed up our feathers to keep the warm air in, and stood on one foot at a time, tucking the other up under our feathers to stop it turning into a claw-shaped ice-cube, but we were still freezing. If I'd had a nose instead of a beak it probably would have been bright red with a dew-drop on the end! The blue skies of the morning were disappearing, and from the west great dark clouds were massing.

'Just as well Taliesin isn't at Cantre'r Gwaelod, T.A.' I said, 'or I might start to worry about Gwyddno Garanhir, him planning a party and all.'

T.A. shivered. 'Oh, don't Tanz! It's bad enough lurking around here waiting for whatever's going to happen without you saying stuff like that. O'Liam's taking his time, isn't he?'

'Well, he's got to find Fliss, get at her, get her out and then come back. Not something you can do in ten minutes, I suppose.'

Just as I finished speaking, O'Liam dropped off the battlements over our heads, squawking furiously. A crossbow bolt missed him by about three inches, and I realised that Jason was still trying to prove his point to Ardwyn.

O'Liam landed in a scurry of feathers. 'I thought my last hour was upon me, I did!' he croaked. 'Taking potshots at me, he is, the lout! Good thing he's not the crack shot he thinks he is!'

'Still, you're back safely,' I said, anxious to know what he had found out. 'Did you find Flissy?'

'I found the dungeon,' he said, preening his feathers back into place. 'And I am of the opinion that your Aunt is inside the thing.'

'Can you get her out?'

'I can, so.'

'Then?' I prompted.

'It might be a tough job. I have to get inside the castle to find the way into the iron dungeon, for there's certainly no other way to get at it. And it crossed my mind, Lady, that a raven is perhaps not the best shape to be flapping around a dungeon in. My imagination shows me pictures of me trapped in a dark corner with a spear sticking out of my vitals.'

'I see your point. I'll need to change you, then, which means we all have to fly up there, and I have to get as close to the iron as I possibly can without it affecting me. Come on, let's get it over with.'

I was actually quite pleased to be doing something. It was getting even colder on the beach, and a thin rain was being driven onshore by the freezing wind. Inside the walls of the castle, however, it was sheltered, and we were able to find a shadowy corner where I could shift the three of us to mice.

'Watch out for the Castell Du cats!' I said, remembering, and O'Liam looked alarmed.

'Oh, Lady, will we get this done quick, now, and leave the place as soon as ever we can,' he squeaked. 'I'm not especially fond of cats even when I'm myself, so to speak.'

We found a flight of steps that were vaguely

familiar, leading downward into darkness. At the bottom we turned a corner and I suddenly felt ill. Flares were stuck into rings on the walls – bronze rings, which weren't what was causing my sickness. I skidded to a stop and put a paw to my whiskers. 'I can't go any further,' I squealed, panicking. 'I can feel the iron.' It was like a great, heavy weight pressing down on me, and I felt weak and hardly able to think.

'Go back round the corner, Lady,' O'Liam said, and shoved me with his small paws. I didn't take much urging. I scampered back and T.A. followed. As soon as I was protected from the iron by the stone walls I felt better.

O'Liam poked his head round. 'I can see the iron doors from here,' he squeaked. 'Fine iron it is, and definitely iron with a great opinion of itself. It might take me some time to make it see reason, so be patient, Lady.'

I didn't have much in the way of patience, but I didn't have much in the way of choice, either. All we could hear at first was O'Liam, squeaking, and then suddenly his whiskery face was poked back round the corner. It looked indignant.

'I think it would be a good idea if you changed me back to myself, Lady,' he said crossly. 'Sure and the iron is making mock of me! Says I'm nothing but a mouse and not O'Liam Ironfinder at all! Says it knows O'Liam Ironfinder personally, for wasn't it me that hunted it down in the first place, and it's certain I'm not he. Change me back at once and I'll teach it who's who, *and* what's what while I'm at it, so!'

I changed mouse to leprechaun, and O'Liam rolled

up his sleeves and marched back around the corner. We seemed to crouch there in the darkness for hours, listening and waiting. We couldn't hear what the leprechaun was saying, but the tone of voice sounded as if he was giving the iron a severe talking-to.

Then we heard the strangest sound. I looked at T.A. and she stared back. 'What do you think that is?' I whispered.

T.A. shrugged. 'A hippopotamus, groaning?' she suggested.

The sound came again. It was a sort of hollow, ringing, hooting sound, like a train whistle but deeper.

'Ah, you good thing!' O'Liam's voice said happily. 'I knew you were a reasonable style of iron all along, so I did.'

And then, around the corner came O'Liam and Flissy. I swiftly changed myself and T.A. back and we had lots of hugs, which made us all feel better.

'How did you get the iron to cooperate?' T.A. asked.

O'Liam blushed, and Aunt Flissy grinned.

'The iron was being a bit difficult at first,' she said, 'apparently it had spent exactly the right amount of time in the furnace to make it extremely big-headed, but O'Liam let it talk itself into a corner and then he threatened it.'

'Threatened it?' I said, bemused. 'How can you threaten iron?'

'Oh, you can, you can,' O'Liam said proudly. 'Don't forget, I've spent my whole life's life dedicated to the stuff entirely. There's but one thing that iron's afraid of, and that's water.'

'Water?' My face must have looked totally blank.

'Think, Tanz. Water plus iron makes rust, right?'

'But O'Liam didn't have any water!'

O'Liam blushed so deeply his golden face turned crimson. Aunty Fliss chuckled. And then I got the picture. And giggled.

'I was improvising, so,' the little man said. 'Maybe I wouldn't have – well, you know – on the iron, but it didn't know that, not at all.'

I gave O'Liam a mighty kiss on the top of his head. 'O'Liam, you're a star. Now, we have to get the others out. Will the iron cooperate and let me go past it?'

'I think it will, Lady. I spoke to it most severely.'

I stuck my nose round the corner, then the rest of me. I felt fine. The four of us ran along the row of barred cell doors, but only Flissy's had been made of iron. The others were made of strong wood with great wooden bolts slotted across, and bronze padlocks. It took only a very small spell to open the shanks and let the prisoners out. Soon I had all the villagers assembled in the long stone passage, including Mali's ancient mother, who may have been a prisoner, but certainly wasn't cowed.

'Just you wait,' she said fiercely. 'I'll get my own back on that tax-collecting, nasty little Henbane person. I'll sort him out soon enough, you see if I don't. I'll teach him the manners his Mam didn't bother with.'

'I'm sure you will,' I soothed her. 'But first we have to get you out of here.'

Sion ap Sion smoothed his bald head and twitched his moustache. 'Not going to be black beetles this time, Lady, I hope?' he said nervously. 'I still has nightmares about being a black beetle, Lady. And then when we was frogs!' He closed his eyes and shuddered. 'Nasty, slimy creatures, frogs. I had horrible thoughts about eating flies while I was a frog. Put me off my dinner for weeks that did.'

'But you are alive because of it, Sion ap Sion,' I reminded him. He opened one eye and surveyed me.

'Aye, I suppose I am.' He sighed. 'So what we going to be this time, then.'

I resisted the urge to turn him into an earthworm and see how he liked *that*. 'Mice, I think.'

And so there we were, around a dozen squeaking, scurrying brown mice. Once again Sion ap Sion's whiskers hadn't co-operated with the spell, so there was one mouse with a fine handlebar moustache . . .

And then I led the way along the passage, up the stairs and into the rapidly gathering twilight. Shadows pooled around the edges of the courtyard, and flares were being lighted by a familiar figure. Ardwyn and Jason had apparently given up taking pot-shots at birds and gone inside.

'Iestyn,' I squeaked, but he didn't hear me. I scuttled across to him and shot up his leg. Startled, he looked down, but by that time I was sitting on his shoulder. 'Iestyn, we've got Flissy out. Now we're going home. So don't worry. She's safe.'

A huge grin spread across his face, and he nodded. 'Where is she, Lady?' he asked.

'Hiding in the shadows, just where that cat is goi –'

I think I probably broke the World Mouse Leaping and Running from a Standing Start record right then. I took off from Iestyn's shoulder and hurtled across to the shadowy corner where eleven cowering, terrified mice had been backed into a corner by a large tabby cat, its body flattened and ready to spring, its tail twitching from side to side. In mid air I changed from mouse to very large and irate buzzard, flexed my wings, spread my dark-barred tail, and with a battle cry of '*pieuoo*' I leapt upon the unsuspecting cat, dug my talons into its back and hauled it into the air. Luckily it was a fairly skinny cat, because the effort of lifting it was horrendous. I heaved it, about three metres off the ground, away from the mice, flew up to an arrow-slit and dropped the furious, squirming, clawing, squalling cat inside. I think I'd picked the guard-room by the terrified screams and bad language that followed me away from the turret.

Then I flew back, shifted them all into owls and we took off. Most of them got into the air without any trouble, but Sion ap Sion couldn't quite achieve lift-off, and was running squawking across the courtyard with his neck stuck out and his wings flapping helplessly. Then, out of the corner of his eye he saw the second cat, a black one with a white front, creeping towards him. It's amazing how quickly he got the hang of flying. He took off just as the cat sprang, and it missed by a feather's breadth.

I flew back to Mali's hut, closely followed by the others, and when we landed outside, shifted them back. Mali's Mam looked twenty years younger.

'Ooh, that was wonderful!' she croaked happily. 'Always wanted to fly, I have, and now I can die happy, 'cause I did it. Look, don't stand hanging about out here. Come in and have a hot drink. Mali, Mali!'

Mali opened the door and flung herself at Dafydd

194

sobbing hysterically. Dafydd clutched her and looked embarrassed.

Mali's Mam prodded her daughter with a bony finger. 'Come on, come on. Pull yourself together, girl. We got guests, save all that soppy stuff for later.'

Wiping her eyes on her pinny, Mali went back into the cottage and we all followed her. The old lady crossed to where Gwydion lay on the bed and stared at him.

'You got him back then, the young Dragon.'

'We did,' Nest said, 'but a fat lot of good it's done us. We can't find a spell to wake him up.'

'Don't expect you could, neither,' the old lady said, her bright eyes flicking from one of us to another. 'Wouldn't have been a spell from round by here, would it? Mali, where's my hot drink?' And the old lady sank happily into her rocking chair and pushed off with her left foot.

Then, suddenly, Flissy squealed. 'Tansy! They're back! Taliesin and Merlin! I can feel them!'

I forgot what the old lady had said and turned to my aunt. 'They are? Where are they?'

'I can't exactly be sure. I can only just feel their auras. I think they're in the west somewhere.'

'That's great,' T.A. said. 'I mean, I'm thrilled we can actually get hold of them now. Look, pardon me for mentioning it, but has anybody thought that the guards at Castell Du might sort of take exception to losing all their prisoners? I mean, one of them might trot down to the dungeons to take a look, right? And find them not there, right? And one of the first places they'll look for them is . . .'

I stared at her. 'Here, right?' I said.

195

23

'You're right, of course,' Nest sighed. 'The question is, where on earth can we go?'

'If Henbane and Maebh weren't there, I'd suggest Cantre'r Gwaelod,' Flissy said, 'but they are, so that's that. Tansy, dear, have you got any ideas?'

I don't often have good ideas, but every now and again – and right now I had one. 'We don't actually have to go far at all, do we?' I said, grinning.

'Well, we can't stay here,' Nest said, frowning. 'First place they'll look will be the village, and then we might as well give up. We'll never get out of Castell Du if they catch us all.'

'But they won't,' I was grinning so hard I must have looked like teeth on legs. 'If we all shift into something else, Henbane won't recognise us, will he?'

'She's right,' T.A. said. 'Good thinking, Tanz. But what?'

'Well, there's one place that we could hide; it's under cover, with lots of company, and plenty to eat. Henbane certainly won't look for us there.'

T.A. gave me a Look.

'All right, all right. We can hide in the beehive back at the *tŷ hir*!'

O'Liam turned pale. 'Sure and we'd be stung to death as quick as summer comes and goes,' he said. 'Bees can give you a terrible time of it. Not the friendliest creatures, bees.' He shivered.

'Only if you steal their honey, O'Liam, not if you are one of them.'

'What, me be a bee? Live in a bee hive?' It wasn't just O'Liam who was staring at me in horror. They all were, all the villagers, Mali, Dafydd, Sion ap Sion. Only Nest, Flissy and Mali's Mam were nodding in agreement. I was getting to like that old lady more and more. I like tough old ladies, and she was tough as old boots.

'Brilliant,' Flissy said. 'Tansy, you go out and ask the bees' permission.'

I slipped out the door and legged it up to the long-house. The sky was dark and wind was lashing the trees. I went over to the little cluster of hives, and felt the first drops of rain.

'Honeybees,' I said, 'I've come to ask a favour . . .'

By the time I got back in, Nest and Flissy had talked the villagers round. After all, if it's a choice between being a bee for a couple of days and being locked up in a dungeon or killed, there isn't really much choice, if you're a sensible sort of person. So I changed unconscious Gwydion into unconscious bee, and carried him cupped gently in my hands while we all trooped through the wood to the *tŷ hir*. Mali's Mam was bright pink with excitement. When we got there I shifted everyone into bees and placed Gwydion, still asleep, on the hive's front doorstep and lastly, shifted myself. A small escort of insects flew out to welcome us in, and a couple more dragged Gwydion inside. I ushered everyone in ahead of me. To my surprise the bees formed two lines in the air, like a sort of guard of honour, and I flew between them.

The hive was warm and sweet-smelling despite the weather, and the background buzz was a contented and

197

strangely comforting sound. We'd be safe for a while. A large bee bustled up and beckoned with its antennae for me to follow it. Mystified, I crawled along behind it, and then suddenly realised I was being taken to meet their Queen.

She was huge, compared to the others, surrounded by honeycomb and bee larvae, and still managed to look totally regal. I did a sort of bee-curtsy and she bowed back. I heard her voice in my head, like the buzzy feeling you get from a dentist's drill, only much more pleasant. Much, much more.

'A thouzzzzand welcomezzz, Lady,' she buzzed. 'An honour it izzz to have you. Zzztay azz long azz you wizzh.'

Afterwards, I went back to the others, who had huddled together. O'Liam didn't look too happy, and Sion ap Sion's moustache, once again, was giving him trouble. I'd ask you to try to imagine a bee with a moustache, but it was traumatic enough seeing it for myself!

We slept the night in the hive, and woke to the busy hum all round us. Bees are single-minded creatures, and as soon as my eyes opened I found myself wanting to buzz off and be busy, too. The lead bees made their way to the entrance to the hive, but then came back disconsolately, because it was raining. It was probably because I had too much time on my hands that I started thinking and putting things together in my mind.

I stretched my wings and then folded them while I idly thought of Taliesin and Merlin – to the west of us, although Fliss hadn't been able to make them hear her yet, which was a major bummer. Then I thought of Gwyddno Garanhir, having a great big party. Lousy weather for it – wet and windy, with a blustery wind howling round the outside of the hive. It would be rough at sea, and I was glad I didn't have to go anywhere . . .

OK, sometimes I'm slow on the uptake, but I get it in the end, all right? I shot into the air, startling Flissy and Nest, who were drowsing. 'Quick,' I yelled. 'Flissy, Nest, *come on!*' And I flew to the opening of the hive, shifted into a seagull, and launched myself into the wind and rain. Once I was free I sat on the roof of the long-house and waited for Flissy and Nest to join me.

'What on earth's the matter, Tansy?' Fliss squawked, stretching her wings out and battling to keep her balance in the near gale-force winds.

'Fliss, Nest,' I said urgently, '*can you reach Taliesin or Merlin yet?*'

They concentrated, and after a few minutes shook their heads. 'No,' Flissy said regretfully, 'it looks as if they've switched off their auras again. They must just have dropped their guard for a while and I got through by accident. Perhaps I caught them just as they landed on the coast, perhaps as they shifted or something like that.'

'Then we have to go to Cantre'r Gawelod,' I squawked.

They looked at me. 'Why?' Nest asked. 'Henbane will be back soon, despite the weather. He daren't leave Castell Du for too long. Once they're back then we can fight them on our terms, not theirs.'

'Don't you realise?' I said, frantically flapping my wings to stay put on the roof, 'put it all together. Cantre'r Gwaelod. Taliesin in the West. Great big storm. *They're all going to drown if we don't warn them!'*

Flissy looked at Nest, Nest looked at Flissy. Grown up, serious looks, and I didn't like them at all.

'If that's going to happen, Tansy,' Flissy said, 'and we know that according to legend some day the land of Cantre'r Gwaelod will disappear in a great storm and everyone in the Sixteen Cities except Taliesin will drown, then it's going to happen. Taliesin told you before Gwydion's Dragonking-making that you can't change history, even if you *are* around before it happens and you know the future. You mustn't even try. If now is the time, then it will happen. Besides,' she said briskly, cocking her head and fixing me with her yellow eye, 'we don't know if Taliesin is there for sure, do we? He could be anywhere on the west coast. And I don't think, in the legend, that Merlin's there at all, and anyway he's magic, so he can get away even if he is there. So don't worry.'

'Don't worry!' I said, *'Don't worry?'* I stared at her, and then at Nest. 'But what about Gwyddno and his wife? Elffin? All the people? Oh, I don't mind if Henbane and Maebh drown, it would be good riddance and solve all our problems, and I know Merlin can take care of himself, but all the others – all the children! I can't just stand by and let all those other people die, Fliss!'

'Yes you can, Tan'ith,' Flissy said sternly. 'You are the Lady, and you must be strong enough to stand aside. What happens will happen. You can't change it.'

200

'I'm going to try, though,' I said. 'Lady or not. And if you won't help me, I'll do it on my own.' And I hurled myself off the roof and into the air, pointed my beak in the general direction of Cantre'r Gwaelod and set off. My eyes were watering so that I could hardly see, and it wasn't entirely the wind in my face.

But I hadn't gone more than a mile or so when I heard a frantic squawk behind me, and looked over my shoulder. It was Flissy, flapping as hard as she could to catch up.

'There's absolutely nothing you can do, Tansy,' she said, 'but I'm coming with you anyway. A family sticks together, right or wrong. Nest is staying behind to look after the others.'

'Thanks, Fliss,' I said. 'We've got to try, right?'

'I promise you it won't make any difference, Tansy. Nothing we can do will save them. What will happen will happen, and you can't change anything. Otherwise there wouldn't be any legends in your time.'

'Blow the legends,' I said fiercely. 'I'm going to give it my best shot anyway.'

Flying into the headwind was exhausting. Instead of being able to swoop and glide on the up-currents and slip down on long slides of air, or better still roost in a field until the storm had blown over, we flew against the terrible wind every flap of the way. Night was coming fast, and at last I stopped in a tree, half dead with tiredness.

'I can't see any more,' I squawked, 'Flissy, we'll have to change into owls if we're going to go any further.'

Seconds later, owl-shaped, fighting the ache of exhaustion in my wings and back, I launched myself once more into the dark sky. Storm clouds tore raggedly across a sky so dark that not a single star could be seen. The moon was stuck solidly behind the cloud, and only occasional glimpses of its light showed us the way. And then I saw the first bolt of lightning zig-zag across the sky, and heard thunder rumbling in the distance. Just when I thought things couldn't get any worse, they did.

No self-respecting owl would fly in conditions like that. It's impossible. Our wings were saturated, and flying rapidly became out of the question. We had no choice but to roost in a tree until the storm passed over. But when the storm passed over, the worst of the weather would, too, and it might be too late.

'We can't afford to wait this out,' I screamed above the howling wind and crashing thunder, 'we have to try another way.' And I side-slipped down out of the tree, and shimmered. I thought 'fox', but something told me wolf would be better, and I found myself in a huge, lithe body covered in coarse grey fur. I howled once at the moon, in misery, pointed my muzzle to the west, and not even looking to see if Flissy was following, loped off towards Cantre'r Gwaelod.

All the time I ran, my four strong legs thudding down on the rain-softened ground, at the back of my mind I heard the words 'no use, no use' running over and over again. We wouldn't get there until after midnight. Would that be too late? Would there be nothing left of the lovely land of Cantre'r Gwaelod, the tall towers of the Sixteen Cities, but a wild and engulfing sea?

At last we came in sight of the hills beyond which lay the Sixteen Cities of Cantre'r Gwaelod. As we climbed them I saw, first, the tallest tower: Taliesin's, and then, as we reached the summit and looked down, all the others. Even in the darkness I could see the city as the lightning glinted on marble and lit up the twisting rivers. We were in time. Just. Swiftly I shifted into an owl again, and launched myself once more into the driving rain and howling wind.

'Flissy, you go and warn Gwyddno. I'll go and wake Seithennyn, the sluice-gate keeper, make him close the gates. Or I'll flipping-well do it myself if he's too sloshed,' I hooted.

I flew at low level across the land, skimming treetops, weaving in and out of tall towers. The sound of harp music came from Gwyddno's palace, and laughter and the chink of wine bottles.

At last, I reached the great sea wall, and flew along it until I reached Seithennyn's hut.

Did you ever feel a total, complete idiot?

Then you'll know exactly how I felt.

The gate was firmly shut, Seithennyn was not only at his post but wide awake and earnestly reading *The Tide Tables of Cantre'r Gwaelod* by flickering rushlight. I'd flown all that way, in terrible weather, for absolutely nothing.

And Flissy, even now, was flying into a banquet where our enemies had been welcomed as honoured guests . . .

Oops.

24

I did a fast U-turn and headed for Gwyddno's palace.
When I got there, it sounded like a good party, but I
had a feeling I wouldn't be enjoying it much. I
swooped past a startled guard and into the Great Hall.
They had all finished eating, if not drinking, and there
were some girls standing in a confused huddle in the
middle of a cleared space next to a long-haired bloke
with a harp, who looked rather peevish at being
interrupted. No one noticed an owl wing it silently
into the roof beams and perch on the layer of dust. I
stifled a sneeze.

Gwyddno sat at the top table with his wife; Maebh
sat on his right, and Henbane beside her. Flissy had
obviously charged into the hall, shifted, and was
standing in front of Gwyddno Garanhir. Henbane was
on his feet, pointing at Flissy.

'This woman is a criminal, my Lord,' Henbane said
smoothly, 'she is a thief and if you will bear with me I
shall have her arrested by my men and taken back
under guard to Castell Du. She will die for this, I
swear. You! Guards! Arrest her, get her out of here!'

The guards glanced at each other and shuffled their
feet nervously. Did they want to try to arrest a witch?
Not unless they fancied spending the rest of their lives
on a waterlily-leaf going, 'ribbit, ribbit', they didn't.

Gwyddno Garanhir, who knew perfectly well who –
and what – Flissy was, made a sort of steeple with his
fingers and tapped his nose with it. I could see that he

was thinking very fast. Elffin, who was sitting on Master Henbane's other side, opened his mouth to protest, but a meaningful glance from his father made him shut it again.

'But Master Henbane,' Gwyddno said, mildly, 'surely you are mistaken. This good lady is Aunt to the Lady of Ynys Haf, one of the Daughters of the Moon, and close to Gwydion Dragonking, who is our rightful King, even if he isn't very much in evidence at the moment. Can't imagine where the boy's gone.'

'Sad to say, he is dead, my Lord,' Henbane said smoothly, not sounding sad in the least, 'but the Amazing, Illustrious, Worshipful Queen Maebh here has agreed to rule this land in his place.'

'By what right?' Elffin was on his feet and shouting, now. Henbane turned to look at him, in much the same way as a snake regards a mouse it is about to eat.

'By every right,' Henbane said. 'Her ancestor was The Lady DisGrace, and she is cousin to the Lady Tan'ith,' (he sort of spat that out) 'seventeen times removed. Therefore in the absence of Dragonking, whom I assure you is not only dead but buried where I doubt his body will ever be found; and of the Lady of Ynys Haf, the half-breed human Tan'ith,' (I could feel myself getting madder and madder) 'then Her Highness Princess Maebh is rightful Queen of Ynys Haf. With myself,' (and here he bowed mockingly) 'as her First Minister, Chief Adviser, Regent and Protector.'

Maebh lowered her thick, dark lashes over her extraordinary blue eyes, produced a set of dimples and managed to turn her ivory skin a delicate pink. Not a freckle in sight, honest. I couldn't help it. I flew down from my rafter to perch on the floor beside Flissy, shifted to myself, and put my hands on my hips.

'Sorry, *Master* Henbane,' I said, 'but you're a bit ahead of yourself. One, Gwydion Dragonking isn't dead and certainly isn't buried anywhere, and two, here I am. The Lady of Ynys Haf. So any time you want to slink off back to Ireland, don't let me keep you. We can all manage perfectly well without you. And her,' I added ungrammatically.

Gwyddno hid a smile. 'This young lady may not look exactly regal, Master Henbane, but I assure you she is indeed the Lady of Ynys Haf.'

Me, not look regal? What was he on about? Then I glanced down. I was back in my ancient jerkin and leather leggings. Drat. Still, clothes weren't important. It was the *poise* and *dignity* of the person inside that counted, right? Still, I wished I'd been wearing something drop-dead tidy. It might have helped a bit, which only goes to proves that Mams can be right sometimes.

Master Henbane sneered. And then his right hand shot out, and a spell hurtled across the room. Fortunately I saw it in time and dodged, and it splattered harmlessly but messily on a tapestry hanging on the wall. Lady Garanhir tutted crossly, most likely worrying whether spell-stains were easy to clean off, being a houseproud sort of person.

I searched around the Spellorium in my head, found an appropriate one (purple frog) and flung it at Henbane. He ducked, and a footman croaked mournfully, sitting on his platter of chicken. Still, I'd sort him out later, poor chap, when I had a spare minute.

I summoned another spell and chucked it, but it missed, and then had to duck, fast, as a fat orange spell whizzed my way. Then Flissy yelled, 'Tan'ith, look out!'

I'd forgotten that Henbane had ordinary soldiers with him. I turned just in time to see a spear launched at my back. Well, I don't hold with violence and bloodshed, especially when it's my blood that's likely to be shed, so I turned it right round on the man who had thrown it, and had the satisfaction of seeing it chase him right round the hall and out the main door, locked on to him like a heat-seeking missile. That'd teach him to try to spear a witch in the back! When I turned round, Maebh was on her feet. The dimples had gone, and Gwyddno and his guests got a glimpse of the real Maebh beneath the good looks. Her face was screwed up, and her small, sharp teeth bared, and she looked as unpleasant as it is possible for a very beautiful person to look.

And then they both started chucking spells at me. Well, up to that point it had been one on one, and even when Maebh joined in, hers weren't up to much, but it was altogether too much for Flissy to put up with, and so she started chucking spells around too. I glanced at her and realised she was thoroughly enjoying herself. Being married to Iestyn, she was trying very hard to be an ordinary-ish mortal because her witchiness made poor Iestyn twitchy. Now she had a chance to be a witch in deadly earnest again.

The trouble was, it really was deadly earnest. The spells that Henbane was hurling were spells that could seriously damage our health and possibly any plans we had for the future, if they hit us. In the end, I started to worry about the number of bystanders who were getting clobbered by the fall-out. Most of them had taken refuge under the tables, but most spells will whiz through wood without even noticing. I decided enough was enough, turned myself into a hobby falcon and hurled my small, anchor-shaped, blue-grey body up to the black beams supporting the roof.

Henbane did likewise, and Maebh stopped hurling spells at Flissy and watched, her mouth open. Henbane perched alongside me, and I waited, tense and ready to take off again, waiting for his next move. I didn't have long to wait: his outline blurred, and became longer and longer, twining round and round the beam, rising and shifting and weaving from side to side. . .

And I was face to face with a king cobra.

Now, in my book that's definitely cheating. We aren't supposed to change into anything that isn't native to Ynys Haf or My Time Wales (the gorillas didn't count: we were between worlds, right?) but there certainly aren't any cobras in Wales, never have been, as far as I know, except in zoos. The trouble was, even as I was indignantly thinking this, the snake was rearing up and spreading its hood with the distinctive pattern, and staring me in the eye. And as just about everyone knows, a king cobra staring a bird in the eye can mesmerise it into keeping still long enough for the snake to strike. I was staring at it like my sister Heledd stares at Whatsisname Crowe when a tiny, bright bird shot up beside us, shimmered – and shifted into a mongoose. This was getting ridiculous. Still, I suppose if Henbane could cheat, so could Flissy. The trouble was, these strange species of creatures were harder to hold on to, because they didn't speak our language, and Henbane sort of melted and fell off the beam, and Flissy, who was a bit blurred round the edges anyway, shifted back rapidly into a yellowhammer and flew down, where she shifted back into herself.

'Thanks, Fliss!' I said, launching myself after Henbane, who was shifting even as he fell. By the time he hit the ground he was a wildcat, and ready to spring as I landed. I shifted into a spider and shot between his legs, and then had a better idea and became a flea . . .

I bit and bit and bit him while I had the chance, but then felt him fizz as he changed and I slipped rapidly back into my own skin. Out of the corner of my eye I saw Gwyddno Garanhir on the edge of his seat with excitement, watching. Better entertainment than the dancing girls, then, I thought, as I changed rapidly into a golden eagle. I spread my massive wings and sort of loomed. *Go on, smartypants,* I thought, *beat that!*

Unfortunately, he did. He turned into a wolf and sprang at me, his slavering jaws wide and red, trying to catch my wing, my neck, any part of me. But his jaws clattered shut on nothing at all, because I wasn't there. I was a black beetle, scuttling like fury for the rushes on the floor under the table. Once hidden, I took the opportunity to get my breath and look around.

I could see Gwyddno Garanhir's feet firmly planted, his wife's (obviously worried by all this wild life scurrying around) tucked up on the rung of her chair, Elffin's planted like his father's, and – Maebh's dainty little white slippers kicked off under the table so that her bare pink pretty toes were wiggling in the air.

I contemplated turning myself into two whole footfulls of verrucas (veruccae? Oh, blow the grammar, I've got a battle to fight), but couldn't quite work out how. Instead I shifted to a large, hairy wolf spider and crawled up her dress, up the skirt, up the bodice, onto her shoulder right next to her ear. Then I started to speak, making my voice sound as close to my memory *of Merch Corryn Du*'s voice as I possibly could.

'*Maebh*,' I hissed in my best spidertalk, '*no good can come of this. Henbane is using you. He wants all your power for himself and then he will kill you. Get away from here. Go and hide somewhere safe until all this is over.*'

'Great-great-great-Granny?' Maebh whispered, startled. 'Aren't you dead?'

'*Of course I'm not, you stupid girl!*' I hissed. '*I'm talking to you now, aren't I? No one can kill me! Not even a dragon. I am Spiderwitch. Now, get out of here while you still can!*' And I leapt from her shoulder onto Lady Garanhir's head.

Maebh didn't need telling twice. She went out of Gwyddno Garanhir's Great Hall like a bat out of hell. Henbane, who had shifted back to himself while he looked for me, watched her go, amazed.

'Come back, you stupid girl!' he yelled. 'Come

back, I tell you! We can beat these paltry little witches!'

But obviously Maebh was more frightened of Spiderwitch than she was of Henbane. She kept going. As she went through the door I saw her shape blur, and a magpie took off into the night sky.

I hopped off Gwyddno's wife's shoulder before she noticed me, and shifted back to myself. 'Just you and me, now, Master Henbane,' I said cheerfully. 'What would you like to try next? Chicken?' And I flapped my arms and made chicken noises.

OK, that was childish, I admit it, but it worked. It made him lose his temper and get careless. His face turned purple with fury, he drew himself up to his full height, conjured up a spell so big he had to hold it in both hands, and he threw it. It was big, and red and ugly. It had the same creepy-crawly look about it as the Grimoire had when it sensed a Badwitch about. If it had hit me I dread to think what might have happened. But Henbane made one big mistake. Instead of summoning up his next spell to zap me with in case that one missed, he was so sure that this one would flatten me permanently that he put his hands on his hips and waited for me to get splatted.

Instead I magicked up a mirror – and turned the spell back on him. Only I doubled its speed. It got him full in the face like a custard pie. He screeched like a banshee, waved his arms and legs about – and began to disappear. First his feet in their fine leather boots went transparent and vanished, and then his knees, his thighs, his body – well, I'm sure you get the idea. The last bit of him to go was his head, his eyes bulging horribly with fury. And then he was gone, I hoped for good. I stared at the spot where he'd been for a short while, to make sure there weren't any spots or dribbles of Henbane left, and then relaxed. I didn't know where he'd gone exactly, but he was definitely Not There.

Flissy gave me a huge hug, and Gwyddno Garanhir settled back in his seat with a huge grin.

'That was the most exciting thing I've seen for years!' he said. 'Now, Flissy dear, before you were so rudely interrupted, what were you saying about floodwater?'

'Floodwater?' Flissy could look more innocent than fresh snow when she wanted to. 'What floodwater? Oh, no, Gwyddno dear. That was just an excuse to get Henbane's attention while the Lady arrived. She's not a very good flier. A bit slow, you know.'

Flissy turned to me and closed her eye in a huge wink. 'Well, Tansy,' she said, smiling. 'Shall we go back? I think Cantre'r Gwaelod will survive a bit longer.'

25

Of course, Gwyddno wouldn't hear of us leaving until the morning, and then we had a large breakfast, so it was gone mid-day when we finally got away. Elffin and Gwyddno couldn't stop talking about the battle that had gone on in their Great Hall, and the footman that had accidentally been turned into a frog was boring all his friends stiff by recounting his adventure over and over.

We flew to the beehive, shifted from birds to bees (confusing, that, if you think about it!) and went in. I thanked the Queen for her hospitality, gathered up our friends and once outside the hive, shifted them back. O'Liam was grinning from ear to ear.

'That obviously wasn't as bad as you'd expected, O'Liam,' I said.

'It was not. Fine, friendly creatures, bees. And a bee in the hive is worth two in the bush. Did we not reach a fair agreement for the future, so?'

I eyed him suspiciously. 'What do you mean?'

'Oh, just a fine, fair sort of a treaty thing involving stings and honey and stuff like that.'

'So long as it's fair to the bees, O'Liam. They are my friends and I don't want them upset.' I could have added 'or cheated' but didn't. After all, O'Liam the Leprechaun was trying to reform. Or so he said.

I explained to the villagers that Henbane and Maebh had been defeated, and got three loud cheers. Then they trooped off to their homes, and we went back into the longhouse, put Gwydion the bee on the bed and shifted him back. He was still snoring loudly.

T.A. sat on a stool beside him, held his hand and talked to him. Nest was grimly mixing a very smelly potion. She didn't look happy.

'What's the matter, Nest?' I asked. 'We've beaten them.'

'How can you say that?' she muttered. 'No, we haven't. Rhiryd ap Rhiryd Goch and his brothers still hold the castle, and Gwydion is still enchanted. We've only just begun.'

'But I chased Maebh away – and totally zapped Henbane,' I protested. 'The others haven't got any magic at all.'

'And where is Henbane?' she asked.

I didn't say anything. I didn't know, did I?

'Exactly,' she said. 'His magic is every bit as powerful as yours – only yours is good and his isn't. Just because you can't see an enemy doesn't mean he's gone. Remember the Spiderwitch. She came back, didn't she?'

'Yes, but –'

'But nothing. Rhiryd and his brothers are still in the castle,' Nest said grimly, 'and Gwydion is still lying there like a loud log, and Merlin and Taliesin are goodness knows where. We aren't out of the woods yet, Tansy.'

I sighed, even though I was sure (wasn't I?) that she was worrying unnecessarily. 'I suppose we aren't. Right. Obviously we haven't managed to find a way to bring Gwydion back yet, but we'll just keep trying until we do, Nest. It has to be there, somewhere, right?'

'Oh, I do hope so, Tansy. In the meantime, we have to do something about Rhiryd Goch. Get him out of the castle so that when Gwydion does come round – if he does – he can get on with ruling Ynys Haf again.'

'It surely won't be too hard to shift that lot. After all, there's nothing magical about them. We can dispose of them, no problem. But first I need to rest and eat –'

'Oh, I like the sound of that,' O'Liam broke in.

'– and then we'll go and clear that nest of rats out of the castle. And then you can have Iestyn back, Aunty Fliss.'

'And about time too.'

The sun was setting behind the castle as we flew towards it, Flissy, T.A. and I. The castle looked black and sinister against the red-streaked sky, and the three of us flapped our rook-wings, tumbling raucously around the sky the way rooks do at sunset, rather enjoying ourselves. After all, it was going to be simple, right? Wrong.

My plan was to fly up to the battlements, shift into myself and go and give Rhiryd Goch, Ardwyn and Jason the fright of their lives. Maybe change them into something totally repulsive. Oh, and send them packing. Sigh. Doesn't always work like that, does it? I should have paid more attention to Nest.

As we flew up and over the battlements, we were met by a rain of missiles being hurled at us – arrows from longbows, shortbows, crossbows, middle-sized bows and any other sort of blooming bow you can think of. Also spears, sticks, stones, rubbish – you name it, it got thrown by any soldier with an arm. Which is something they all had two of.

We dodged and got out of there, fast. So fast, T.A. flew head-on into a tree.

'That hurt,' she grumbled, closing one eye and squinting downwards. 'I'm sure I've bent my beak.'

'I think,' I said unnecessarily, 'they were expecting us. Ardwyn and Jason's aim hasn't improved much, but there are apparently a lot of pretty good shots among the castle guard, darn it.'

We sat in our tree and watched. Everything that flew over, round or generally near the castle was getting blasted. I watched a blackbird plummet to the ground with a crossbow quarrel through it, and moaned, quietly. Then I remembered who I was and sent out a general warning to all creatures to stay away from Castell Du until this was over. Within seconds the sky was clear, and I threw a spell that healed the blackbird. It flew groggily away.

'It's no good,' I said at last. 'We'll have to try again tomorrow.' And we flew disconsolately back to the long-house and sat around the fire trying to think of some way we could get inside the castle.

Every now and again I'm really glad T.A. is involved in this, even though it is a huge risk to bring her to Ynys Haf, her being totally mortal and not half-and-half like me. She has a totally mortal brain, you see, and therefore (sometimes) it works in a totally mortal way and comes up with a logical answer.

'Tanz,' she said, when we were lying side by side on our pallets on top of the long-house platform, 'you know you can't get into the castle because everyone is expecting you to come in as a bird or something?'

'Yes,' I yawned. 'That's the whole problem, T.A.'

'Exactly,' she said, propping herself up on one elbow. 'Then why don't you try getting inside as a mortal? Not as a bird, or a bluebottle or a cat, but as a human being? After all, other people are going in and out all the time. Why not us?'

I sat up and stared at her. 'T.A., you might have hit on something! I don't know if it will work, but it's certainly worth a try.'

And so, next morning, we tried. We started out early and walked to the castle, and in the little wood outside the main gate, I magicked each of us some serving-wench clothes just like the ones Mali wore to work. And then we waited until Mali and some of the other servants who lived outside the castle arrived for work. As they passed us, we slipped in amongst them, and chatted to Mali, who seemed to have got some courage from her tough old Mam and didn't descend into gibbering terror as she would have done in the past.

We crossed over the drawbridge, our feet thudding on the wooden planks, and then we were inside, all three of us. We didn't look at each other, but I could feel T.A.'s smug grin without seeing it.

The others went to the various places in the castle where they worked: the stables, the kitchens, the various towers and turrets, and the three of us slipped into the main tower, through the Great Hall and through the door at the far end where Henbane and Maebh had taken up residence. And then I heard Maebh's voice.

'Of course I ran. You would have run too, if you'd heard it. It was my Great-great-great-Granny's voice, I tell you. She told me to run, and I did. Whatever Granny tells me to do, I do it, quick. I don't know why you're picking on me. It isn't my fault.' And she began to sniffle. I told T.A. and Flissy to stay back, and I went and stuck my eye to the door of Maebh's room. It was draughty, and made my eye water, but I could see her, patting the corners of her eyes with a dainty handkerchief. She even cried prettily, that one. No wonder I couldn't take to her. But who was she talking to? Whoever it was, he was invisible . . .

Oh, no. If it was Henbane, then I'd only made matters worse by turning his own spell back on him. An invisible enemy would be almost impossible to fight. But then I heard another voice, and realised that it wasn't Henbane's silky Irish tones, but a rougher, harder Welsh voice. The speaker came into view, and a shiver went down my spine as I recognised Rhiryd ap Rhiryd Goch. But I'd beaten his father, and I'd beat him and his brothers too, somehow.

So it was still Maebh, then. Only Maebh. I really hadn't thought that she had the courage to come back and fight us, not once I'd sent her packing, but obviously I was wrong.

Then, suddenly, I felt magic around somewhere. My bones were sensing it. Strong magic. But whose? Oh no, not Henbane . . .

I crept back to the others and reported.

'Maebh?' Flissy said. 'She isn't that powerful, Tansy. Maybe you're imagining it. Maebh won't be hard to handle now that we're inside, I'm sure. And as for Rhiryd – Rhiryd needs a long time in a dungeon somewhere. That'd teach him a lesson.'

218

'Gwydion doesn't agree with dungeons,' I said, sadly.

'At the moment, Tan'ith,' Flissy reminded me, 'Gwydion isn't around to make decisions. It's up to you what happens to Rhiryd and his brothers.'

'Let's sort out Maebh first, all right?' I suggested. T.A.'s face was pink with excitement, but I could tell she was nervous. 'Look, T.A.,' I said, patting her arm, 'you don't need to get involved in this. You can wait outside until it's all over if you like.'

'You have got to be joking!' she said, staring at me in disbelief. 'I wouldn't miss this for anything, Tanz!'

'Then try to keep out of the way, dear,' Flissy said gently. 'There may be a lot of nasty spells flying around, and we don't want you accidentally hit.'

As silently as I could manage, I lifted the latch on the door and pushed it open. Rhiryd's back was towards us, but Maebh saw the movement and was staring straight at me when we went through the door. She squeaked and her hands flew up to cover her mouth.

'Oh!' she yelped, 'she's here, she's here, she is!'

'Who?' Rhiryd Goch stared at her, and then slowly turned. 'You!' he said, his eyes narrowing. Even close up he was horribly like his father. His face was thinner, and less lined, of course, but the foxy hair and stocky body were just like his father's. His character was pretty similar, too, from the expression on his face. His hand flew to his sword, and he drew it, advancing on us.

I swiftly turned the sword into a banana. Yes, I know, bananas don't grow in Ynys Haf or Wales, but it was the first thing I thought of, all right? 'You,' I said sternly, pointing my finger at him, 'keep quiet, or else. You,' I turned my accusing digit on Maebh, 'I thought I told you to run.'

'You never did. It was – oh.' Her face fell.

'I got rid of your Granny once and for all, Maebh. Last I saw of Spiderwitch she was heading for the mountains dangling from the talons of a very large dragon. A red one,' I added. 'Fiercest of the lot. Welsh, you know. Your Granny is gone forever.'

Maebh's pretty face contorted and became ugly with rage. Suddenly she sprang into the air and became Astarte's magpie, huge, its glossy black wings spread, the savage beak aimed at my eyes. I threw a spell and it hit her in mid-air. I expected her to disappear, but instead she shivered, the magpie's outline wavered – and standing in front of me was the Spiderwitch. OK, my mouth fell open and Flissy and T.A. gasped. None of us were expecting Spiderwitch. I'd really, really thought that she was gone for good. Before I could even begin to re-think my tactics, the outline shimmered again, and she was Astarte. I began to feel a bit shell-shocked. Exactly who – or what – was I up against, here? The outline shimmered again, and Maebh was back.

I realised suddenly that the shape-shifts were just a fairly weak illusion. *She didn't have the power to make the changes stick!* She wasn't strong enough. And while she might be able to shift into the *look* of Spiderwitch and Astarte, she didn't have the powers that went with their shapes. I folded my arms and frowned at her. Should I warn her off and let her go?

Or finish her entirely by changing her into something without enough brain to be a danger ever again? After all, she hadn't had much of a one to start with.

And then I felt that strange, magical sort of nudge again. There was powerful magic somewhere close, I could feel it in my bones.

'Maebh,' I said sternly. 'You aren't strong enough to fight me. Someone else is here. Someone powerful. So who is it?'

Maebh produced her hanky again. 'No one, I swear, Lady. Oh, please forgive me and let me go.' The tears started to gush again. Honestly, she'd drown a fair-sized city, this one. She was such a wimp!

'But I know you're lying, Maebh,' I said. 'And I shall turn you into something quite disgusting – a slug or a head-louse – unless you tell me the truth. Tell me, who is it?'

'But I don't know, I tell you!' Maebh shrieked. 'Please, Lady, please don't turn me into a slug.'

'A slug you will be, unless you tell me who it is!' I glared at her threateningly. 'Come on, you must know. Who is it?'

A silky, familiar – and ever so slightly sinister – voice spoke from behind me.

'She isn't lying, Tan'ith. But think. Who else could it be? It's me, of course!'

26

I swung around. There was no one there except Flissy and T.A., both looking confused and a bit scared. Henbane! It had to be. Darn it, why had I gone and invisible-ised him? An enemy I couldn't see was seriously scary.

'Henbane?' I said, 'show yourself, you coward!'

But then I realised that it hadn't been Henbane's voice.

The air in front of me began to shimmer, like a heat-haze on a country road. In the haze there was a tall shape, and I stared, trying to make out the figure. It wasn't Henbane, it was too tall. And then I recognised him.

'Merlin?' I didn't believe it. '*Merlin?*' I started to get cross. 'But Merlin, you're on our side! You're one of the good guys! You can't be behind Maebh!'

Merlin, nattily dressed in Levis and a World Tour 2040 T-shirt for a rock band called 'Excalibur', dusted himself off and frowned. 'I'm not *behind* anyone, Tan'ith,' he said loftily, swapping his trendy shades for round little glasses. 'And I'm not *in front of* anyone, either. I am Merlin, Necromancer. I just *am.*'

Aunty Fliss was staring at him suspiciously. 'Merlin? What's going on? Where do you fit in all this?'

'Where do I fit? I devised the whole thing, of course.' He took a mirror and a comb out of the air and, having combed his hair, dropped them. They vanished before they hit the floor.

'Devised? You make it sound like a computer game or something. Are you telling me that Henbane and Maebh's take-over bid for Ynys Haf is up to you?'

'Oh good grief! Of course not. That was entirely that wretch Henbane's idea. I just took advantage of it.'

I was almost lost for words. 'And what about Gwydion? Was it you who kidnapped him and put an enchantment on him and shut him up in the Time Door?'

'No. That was Henbane, too. And the girl . . . Maebh doesn't have much of a brain, but she's pretty enough to lead an army anywhere. Was another girl like that, once,' he mused. 'Helen somebody or other. Real corker. Face that launched a –'

'Thousand ships. I heard,' I said crossly. 'So, explain, please.' I had sort of forgotten that the person I was eyeball to eyeball with was Great Merlin, Gwydion's tutor, who could probably vaporise me with his little finger. I just wanted to find out what on earth was going on.

'Once Henbane arrived with Maebh and she bewitched Gwydion –'

'What do you mean, bewitched? You said she didn't have much in the way of magic!'

'There are other ways of bewitching, Tan'ith,' Merlin said loftily, 'not all to do with magic. And she *is* very pretty. But the spell is down to Henbane.'

'Hmph.' I didn't like the sound of *that*. 'So, then what?'

'Taliesin was all for pitching in and sorting things out, taking the enchantment off Gwydion and giving him a good talking to.' Merlin raised his forefinger and wagged it at me. 'But I decided that it would be a good test for you. To see if you are worthy.'

'Worthy?' I felt rather as if I might explode any minute. '*Worthy?* What of, for goodness sake?'

He gazed at me pityingly. 'Why, of being Gwydion's Queen, of course. You are half-human, Tan'ith, and even though legend says –'

'Legend my asterisk!' I said furiously. 'Did anyone ask me if I want to be Queen? Did Gwydion? Did you? No. So what right have you to, to –'

'Every right, Tan'ith. Because if you are not fit to be Queen, then Gwydion, sadly, may not be Dragonking.'

I stared at him. 'What? But he is! You crowned him yourself. How can he not be?'

'Ah, but Maebh's claim to Ynys Haf is a strong one. And if Gwydion is stuck in a spell, then he can hardly be Dragonking, can he? And you haven't managed to remove it yet, so the enchantment stands. And if he is asleep, he can hardly rule anything. Except possibly his dreams.' Merlin sighed. Even in my fury, I realised that although he was on Gwydion's side, he was the Great Steward of Ynys Haf, and regardless of anything or anyone else, Ynys Haf was his major responsibility. I was beginning to understand. Merlin was a sort of natural force. Like the wind, or lightning.

'So,' I said slowly, 'let me get this straight. Once Henbane and Maebh moved in, and Gwydion was kidnapped and enchanted, you sort of took advantage of the situation to set me up to sort things out. Right?' My teeth, by now, were firmly gritted. T.A. was watching me the way people who live under volcanoes watch for fizzy smoke.

'Right.' Merlin pulled up a chair and sat on it, the wrong way round, so that his folded arms rested on the high back. His eyes, behind the round lenses, didn't leave my face.

'So, you knew what would happen, right?'

'Right. I know everything. Before it happens, naturally.'

'Couldn't you have stopped it happening?'

Merlin spread out his large hands. 'Of course not. Can you stop the earth turning?'

'But you could have helped me – with Big Deirdre, and Conor of the Land Beneath, and in the battle with Master Henbane?'

'I could have. But what point would there have been? What sort of a test would it have been if I had helped you? In fairness there were a few times when I had to restrain Taliesin, who seems to be quite fond of you for some reason, but he saw reason in the end. He had to. I turned him into one of his own harps. It didn't keep him quiet, but at least his complaints were musical. Which reminds me – I must get round to turning him back. Besides,' he went on, 'you managed without help, didn't you?'

My fury was beginning to subside. Not much, though. I still thought he had a hell of a cheek to think that he could test me out for a job no one had ever asked me if I wanted. Not even Gwydion. (*But he did kiss you*, my brain said, so I told it to shut up. So he kissed me. So what?)

'Were Nest and Flissy in on this?'

225

Merlin looked shocked. 'Blooming Bendigeidfran, no! They would certainly have spoiled the whole thing somehow. They're on your side, you silly girl, and besides, they're female and sentimental. It's only I, the Great Merlin, who can be completely aloof, unbiased and disinterested. Because, you see, I just Am.'

Earth, air, fire and water. 'So, did I pass your test?'

'Almost.'

'Almost?' I shrieked. 'For goodness sake, what else do I have to do? I've beaten Henbane and Maebh, rescued the villagers, recaptured Castell Du – well, near as dammit – what did I do wrong? What more do I have to do?'

'Well, as to what you did wrong, first you liberated a leprechaun and brought him to Ynys Haf – but that might be a blessing in disguise, we'll see – and secondly Henbane has disappeared but not exactly gone, and third, Gwydion is still under his enchantment. So, no. You haven't passed the test completely. Yet.'

I suddenly noticed Rhiryd ap Rhiryd Goch trying to sneak out of the chamber on his little tippy toes. 'You. Stop. Now.' He stopped and turned round. 'Sit,' I pointed to a chair. He sat. I turned my attention back to Merlin.

'O'Liam saved our lives. I couldn't leave him for Conor to punish. And I'll get Gwydion sorted out. Somehow.'

'And what do you propose to do with this chap?' Merlin jerked his head in Rhiryd's direction. 'And his unpleasant little brothers.'

Because I was thoroughly unsettled by Merlin's

226

revelations – a big part of me was still feeling 'how dare he?' – I probably acted without thinking. Well, I did, actually. I concentrated hard, sent some thought-waves off to find Ardwyn and Jason, and fetched them. At a run. At a hop, actually, in Jason's case, because he was trying to put his trousers on and only had one leg in.

When I had their full attention, and all three brothers were lined up in front of me, I folded my arms and gave them a Hard Stare. 'The way I see it, gentlemen, you have two choices. Either you stay here and annoy me, in which case I shall turn you all into something smaller and slimier than you already are, or you agree to disappear and go back to the Out Isles or the Lost Lands or wherever you came from, and never come back to Ynys Haf again. Ever.'

They considered their options for all of fifteen seconds, and then went. So fast that they actually got stuck in the door trying all three to go through it at once. Merlin tutted under his breath, and shook his head pityingly, although I wasn't sure if it was at them or me.

'Now, Maebh,' I said. She started to cry again. 'Look, you've probably had a lousy life, one way and another,' I said, helplessly. I hated to see anyone cry, even Maebh. 'First being brought up by Spiderwitch, then having to hang around dreadful Astarte, being a magpie all the time, then getting used by Henbane, and now being bullied by Rhiryd, who is a thoroughly Bad Lot just like his father was. If I let you go, will you promise to behave and never bother me again?'

She nodded (prettily) through her tears and managed a dimpling, watery smile.

'Oh, all right. Go on then. But remember. Any trouble and you'll be sorry.'

She didn't need telling twice. She must have been the fastest magpie on the planet. Merlin raised his eyes to the rafters and sighed.

'What?'

'Oh, nothing. It's just that you have rather a short memory. And I think she had her fingers crossed behind her back.'

'She wouldn't dare, I said, crossly. 'Come on, let's go home and find a way of de-enchanting Gwydion.'

Back at the *tŷ hir* I was delighted to find a large silver harp which Merlin turned back into Taliesin, who gave me a huge hug, and the great wolfhounds, Bran and Garan, who stood on their hairy hind legs and washed me thoroughly. They'd already done the same to Nest and T.A., and also to Gwydion by the number of dog hairs all over him. O'Liam, who was about one-third of the size of the wolf-hounds, had taken himself up the ladder to the sleeping loft for safety, and was sitting on the edge, the green and gold slippers dangling.

I looked down at the peacefully slumbering Dragonking and sighed. I was absolutely certain that there were no more spells in the Spellorium that I could possibly try. Flissy had said that there was nothing left in the Physicians of Myddfai's book, and Nest had tried every recipe and spell she could possibly think of, and one or two I think she invented. Then I noticed that Merlin and Taliesin were staring at me expectantly.

'You *know*!' I said accusingly. 'You know perfectly

228

well how to release Gwydion, don't you? And you aren't telling me, are you?'

Taliesin opened his mouth but Merlin scowled at him and he shut it again. 'You have the answer already, Tan'ith,' Merlin said mildly. 'The end is in the beginning. To paraphrase what that tiresome Queen of Scots person once said.'

Was there anyone Merlin didn't know? Probably not. So, it was down to me, then. Right. Start at the beginning, Tanz, I told myself. First find out who put the spell on Gwydion. Well, it wasn't Merlin, and I knew Taliesin wouldn't, so it must have been Henbane or Maebh. Maebh certainly wasn't strong enough, so it had to be Henbane. So why couldn't we find a way of taking off the enchantment? Where were we going wrong? A spell, surely, was a spell, was a spell, was a spell, right? What was different about an Irish spell and a Welsh one? I sighed. Magic was *hard* sometimes.

And then it hit me. I remembered what O'Liam had said, and what Mali's old Mam had hinted. *It wasn't the spell. It was the language!*

'Oh, O'Liam, dear,' I called sweetly. 'Could you come down here a minute, please?' Merlin became suddenly still and watchful.

'No, indeed I could not. One of them great hairy beasts will gobble me up entirely, so it will. Will I talk to you from up here, instead?' And he drew his little legs up in case Bran or Garan jumped up and dragged him down.

'Taliesin, will you please put the dogs outside for a while?' I asked. Taliesin whistled and the dogs followed him outside. Then he came back in and shut the door.

'Will you come down now, O'Liam, please?' I asked.

'Are you certain they can't break down that flimsy old door?' he asked nervously. 'Big as old hairy elephants them dogs are, if not bigger.'

'That door would keep Big Deirdre out, O'Liam. Come down.'

Nervously, one eye on the door, O'Liam came slowly down the loft-ladder.

'O'Liam. You see the Dragonking over there, fast asleep?'

'Oh, I do so.'

'And you know that an enchantment was put upon him?'

'I do, so.'

'And you know that all our Welsh spells can't remove it?'

'That I do.'

'But tell me, O'Liam. Would an Irish spell remove an Irish enchantment?'

He grinned, his little pointed face shining. 'It would so, Lady. You had only to ask.' I wanted to throttle him, rather, but fought it down, because he was a leprechaun, and couldn't help being sneaky. It was in his blood and as he said, a leprechaun doesn't change its spots.

'As a favour to me, O'Liam, will you try, please?'

'I will so. Would there be any of them chippety things in it?'

'Afterwards, O'Liam. Gwydion first.'

O'Liam sat beside Gwydion and put one small, golden hand on the dark forehead.

'Duine atá i do chodladh, aithnim duit muscailt
Tarraingt anáil mhór amháin
Duine atá i do Chodladh, aithnim duit muscailt.'

Magically, I heard the words in my own language as O'Liam spoke them:

'Sleeper, I ask you to wake
One full breath do take
Sleeper, I bid you wake.'

I crossed my fingers, crossed my eyes, crossed just about everything. For a moment, nothing happened, and then – Gwydion took a huge breath in, opened his eyes and stretched. He yawned and swung his legs over the side of the low bed. And caught sight of all of us staring at him.

'Tanz? T.A.? What are you doing here? Merlin? What on earth's going on? What are you staring at?'

'It's a long story, Gwyd,' I said, a great big grin spreading across my face. 'But first, I have a meal to magic.'

T.A and I stayed a day or two longer, enjoying Ynys Haf. The villagers were overjoyed to have Gwydion back in Castell Du, and I had a few fairly sharp words to say to him about Maebh. I expect you can guess what. But then the time came, as it always does, for us to leave my lovely Island of Summer and go back to Our Time. And school.

231

T.A. and I had joined Gwydion, Merlin and Taliesin in Castell Du, and the night before we left everyone – even T.A., who isn't famous for her tact – left us alone beside the fire in Gwydion's private solar room. O'Liam Ironfinder, O'Liam of the Green Boots, O'Liam DragonRouser as he lately called himself, now installed in Castell Du as First Leprechaun to the Dragonking, was full up and snoring in his sleeping bag in his own room, and Gwydion and I sat side by side on footstools beside the great, blazing hearth.

'I wish you didn't have to go back, Tanz,' he said, picking up my hand and playing with my fingers.

'I have to go, Gwydion,' I said. 'I've got exams to sit, and colleges to apply to.'

'The Dragonqueen of Ynys Haf doesn't need college.'

'Maybe not. But I do. I need the best education I can get, Gwydion. I need to learn how not to make mistakes.'

'You didn't make any mistakes. You saved Ynys Haf.'

'Mainly by accident, Gwyd. Besides, I don't remember anyone ever asking me to be Queen of anything, let alone Ynys Haf.'

He looked at me blankly. 'But you don't need to be asked, surely? It's in the legend: "The seventh daughter of the seventh daughter of the two-hundred-and-seventy-seventh generation of the Daughters of the Moon will be Queen to the two-hundred-and-twenty-second Dragonking of Ynys Haf."' You're it, and so am I.'

'Oh, well, that's settled, then, is it?' I said sarcastically. 'Except I never heard that legend.'

'Oh, good grief, stop arguing, woman!' And he grabbed me and kissed me. And no, I'm not telling you if he did it again. So there. It's private.

27

I didn't want to go back. But I did. T.A. and I, hand in hand, hugged everybody – Merlin included, although at times I still wanted to smack him very hard or kick his shins or something – and Gwydion gave me an extra special hug and kissed me somewhere in the region of my left ear. Then we stepped into the Door in Time. Much to my surprise, we emerged, very windblown, in the car park at Portmeirion, right next to our car.

We were quiet driving home, T.A. and I, lost in our own thoughts. Mam and Dad still weren't back, and T.A.'s Mum hadn't even missed her when she rang home. Fflur sniffed me comprehensively, recognising Bran and Garan's smell, and licked me until I was soggy from head to toe. We had some beans on toast, and then went and sat on the back step in the sunshine, talking, Fflur lying at our feet.

T.A. picked up a pebble and tossed it. It landed about six inches from Fflur's nose. She lazily opened an eye and shut it again, obviously deciding it was too hot to bother.

'It must be incredibly weird, being you, Tanz,' T.A. said, scuffing her bare foot in the grass.

'Weird? Why?' I stared at her.

'Well, for a start you're a witch, but that's not what I mean. I've got used to that, sort of. No, it's –' she stopped.

'What?'

'Well, here's me, just finished my GCSEs –'

'Straight As and A-stars, you jammy so-and-so,' I said.

'I worked for them, didn't I?'

'So did I, but I didn't get straight As.'

'Anyway,' she went on, 'GCSEs, then A levels, college, working somewhere, I suppose, maybe even get married when I'm really old, and then there's you.'

'Same as you, I suppose,' I said, not thinking straight.

'Except you've got this whole parallel universe life sort of thing. If you don't like what's happening in this time, you can just pop off and go be Dragonqueen.'

'Yes, but –'

'But nothing, Tanz. It's all mapped out for you. Good grief, Merlin's actually tested you on it!'

'And don't think I've forgiven him yet, because I haven't,' I said, grimly.

'But don't you ever wonder why you're bothering to study for A levels and stuff?'

'Often,' I said, 'but it's got more to do with being lousy at exams than it has with Ynys Haf. But I see what you're getting at, T.A.'

'Well then.'

'Well then what? I'm not seventeen yet, for goodness sake, and I'm supposed to think about all that? One thing I've learned: time is so different in Ynys Haf that I reckon I've got all the time in the world to do what I want here in my time – all the girly stuff, and my education and that. If I ever feel I'm ready for Ynys Haf, then I'll go, and Gwydion will be waiting, right?'

235

T.A. grinned and thumped me on the arm. 'Good. I really, really want us to go off to college together.'

'Fingers crossed and A levels willing,' I said glumly. 'I don't intend to go back to Ynys Haf again until I've finished those, anyway.'

Me and my big mouth, right?

Suddenly Fflur leapt to her feet, barking loudly, and I looked up. A bird was fluttering towards us, a pigeon, obviously exhausted by the look of it.

'Grab it, T.A.,' I said, holding Fflur's collar tightly. She caught it in mid-air, and the creature relaxed into her hands, its head drooping. It looked oddly familiar . . .

'There's a message on its leg, Tanz,' she said.

She unrolled the tiny note, and then looked at me. 'Oh, Tanz,' she said. Her face was pale.

'What?'

She held out the paper, and I took it. In tiny, crabbed brown writing, that looked as if the ink had somehow been made of the earth itself, were the words:

To the Lady Tan'ith of Ynys Haf:
You stole O'Liam Ironfinder from me, and you gave me a promise. By all the Laws of all the Kingdoms of All the World, you have a Promise to keep and amends to make.

Ni dhiolann dearmhad fiacha

Forgetting a debt does not pay it.

It was signed with a big, wobbly cross, and underneath was written

The mark of Conor, Lord of the Land Beneath.

HERE ENDS THE FIRST BOOK OF TANITH.

Many, many thanks to Maria Rodgers,
who provided the Erse translations.

My apologies to every Irish person on the planet –
I have tried to make O'Liam of the Green Boots as
un-Oirish and Begorrah-ish as I possibly could.
If I haven't succeeded, I'm afraid it's my fault!
But I tried, I tried!

JENNY SULLIVAN

THE BACK END OF NOWHERE

Jenny Sullivan

sb   £4.95   1 85902 497 1

For Catrin Morgan of Pennsylvania, U.S.A., the new
factory that her father has to open up in Wales means
tragedy. It means leaving her normal life in America,
leaving her best friend, leaving her place as cheerleader for
someone else to fill and, worst of all, leaving her almost-
boyfriend, Kurt. To go where? The Back End of Nowhere,
that's where. Wales, where she'll have to live in a house
full of antiques and go to school in *uniform!* Her father
thinks it's all so wonderful—the land of his ancestors,
history and all that. What on earth is Catrin supposed to
make of those old Welsh legends—of the sea-harp, the
sky-egg and the earthstone?

FOLLOWING BLUE WATER

Jenny Sullivan

sb   £4.95   1 85902 732 6

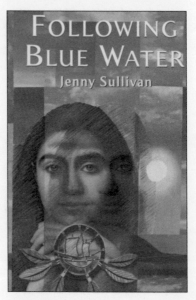

The summer before college should be a special one — school life left
behind, a long holiday stretching ahead for doing nothing but slopping
around and dreaming of the future.

But for Angharad, it's not quite like that.
Her mother chooses this year — of all years!
— to go backpacking in India, bundling Angharad off to North Wales
to stay with her father and a bunch of arty people who'll (probably)
expect her to tend on them hand and foot.

There's no doubt that it's a time when Angharad needs a friend —
a *good* friend; possibly male. Possibly more than one . . .